*This book is dedicated to Sarah Harrison
and her charity Sarah's Star.
(http://www.sarahs-star.org)*

The Bar at the Bottom of Broadway

By

Conor Sharkey

MAPLE
PUBLISHERS

The Bar at the Bottom of Broadway

Author: Conor Sharkey

Copyright © Conor Sharkey (2025)

The right of Conor Sharkey to be identified as author of this work has been asserted by the author in accordance with section 77 and 78 of the Copyright, Designs and Patents Act 1988.

First Published in 2025

ISBN 978-1-83538-861-7 (Paperback)
        978-1-83538-862-4 (E-Book)

Cover Design and Book Layout by:
        Maple Publishers
        www.maplepublishers.com

Published by:
        Maple Publishers
        Fairbourne Drive, Atterbury,
        Milton Keynes,
        MK10 9RG, UK
        www.maplepublishers.com

CONTENTS

Chapter One

As the blood splashed across the pillars of pint glasses Shaun Donnelly decided this was his last shift in The Barking Dog.

He was getting out. And not just out of the pub but out of Ballyrush.

Mickey Kinneally roared in pain as he held his face where Frankie Ferguson had just glassed him. The slice down his left cheek was deep and was going to require several stitches.

It was the latest episode in a nasty feud that had erupted between rival gangs in the town, one that had so far seen a man shot in the ankles, another battered into a coma, a petrol bomb hurled through the window of a house and a car belonging to a local councillor torched.

To anyone with half a brain the reasons for the feud were obvious - drugs. But this was the new Northern Ireland, one that eight years earlier had captured international respect with the signing of the so-called 'Good Friday Agreement'.

And in the new Northern Ireland nothing was straight forward.

Applause had rung out around the world when it was declared that the paramilitary organisations responsible for decades of violence were leaving the stage for good.

Leaving the stage.

It was a strange way to describe it, Shaun Donnelly, or 'Loaf' as he was only ever known, thought. Like they were characters in a musical, enjoying a standing ovation before taking a bow and walking off together.

Following the signing of the peace deal, money had poured in from Europe and America.

Overnight, or at least that's how it felt, the ominous border crossings and military sangers that had for so long darkened Northern Ireland's landscape had started to come down.

A brighter future, both literally and metaphorically.

Within months of pen being put to paper diggers had appeared to begin work on multi-million pound road and bypass projects.

Community centres started popping up, play parks were developed and public art was suddenly a thing in towns and villages more accustomed to petrol bombs and police raids.

In Derry there was talk of some sort of peace bridge while in Belfast plans were being created for a 'Titanic Quarter' to highlight the city's links to the doomed liner.

A new vocabulary had found its way into the Northern Ireland dictionary in the years since the 1998 Agreement too. Phrases like 'devolved powers', 'cross-border co-operation' and 'all-Ireland connectivity' were now embedded in the lexicon, spoken on the evening news bulletins like they had always been there.

To those on the outside, all was finally well on the little island.

For those actually living in the new world the reality was more complicated. And it was why Loaf Donnelly's Saturday night was being spent having to deal with these two wankers, currently being dragged out the door of The Barking Dog screaming that they would shoot each other.

'I've had enough of this Patsy. I'm done,' he remarked to his work colleague when the furore finally started to die down.

'Me too Loaf, me too. What are you going to do?'

'I'm jacking it in. Remember that other job I was telling you about? I'm going to take it.'

'Good for you kid. I'll be sorry to see you go but I don't blame you one bit.'

Patsy continued, 'It never used to be like this you know. This used to be a lovely place to come for a quiet pint. Now it's just drama every week. Last Friday evening it was that halfwit Angelo McHugh going bananas because he put £150 in the poker machine. Now this. It's not worth it, it's just not worth the hassle anymore.'

Outside the air was alive with sirens, both ambulance and police. As the squad cars began to arrive, the crowd that had gathered began to drift off. They knew the PSNI would be trying to round people up to make statements about what they had witnessed. And in a town like Ballyrush speaking to the cops could seriously damage your health. Besides, who wanted to spend their Saturday evening chatting to the plod?

The Barking Dog was nearly empty when its owner, Denzel Walsh, came dashing through the door.

'What's happened here lads,' he asked breathlessly. 'I got a call to say there had been a row.'

Pulling out bar stools so he could mop up the cocktail of blood and beer that had pooled on the floor, Loaf explained, 'Frankie Ferguson hit Kineally with a glass. Got him good too, he's going to have a nasty scar when it's healed.'

'What was it about?'

'You know what it was about Denzel. Didn't I tell you months ago there was going to be a dust up? You've seen the shit that's been happening over on Springdale Estate, cars hijacked, threats daubed on walls. I told you to put security on the door but you were too miserable to hire a bouncer. And now look where you are, with an empty pub and the whole town chatting about you.'

Patsy Devlin, who had worked in The Barking Dog for over 35 years, smiled a secret smile to himself. It wasn't often Denzel

Walsh, one of Ballyrush's most prominent businessmen, was served up hard truths like this.

'Young Donnelly, if this is such a terrible place to work why don't you go and find shifts somewhere else? I hear Maurice over in The Townhouse is looking for staff. You can finish up here this evening and don't bother coming back. Me and Patsy will manage just fine without you.'

Before Loaf could snap back that he was leaving anyway, Patsy jumped in with an unexpected announcement.

'Actually Denzel I think I'm going to call it quits too,' said the older man as he shoved a tray full of bloodied pint pots into the glasswasher.

'Ah Jesus Patsy, would you wind your neck in. You've been pulling pints since the Pope was an altar boy, what are you going to do with yourself if you aren't working here?'

'I'll slip quietly and happily into retirement Denzel, that's what I'll do. I'm 66 next birthday, the pension is just around the corner. My Annie has finished up at the school so we'll have her retirement money coming in too. I'd say we'll manage just fine.'

'Patsy, you and I have been friends for how long, 30 years and more? And this is how it ends?'

'Denzel, you don't know what it's like in here anymore because you're never here. You're always drinking coffee with the other big business knobs in the town or you're away playing golf in Lanzarote. Loaf is right, one of these days Kinneally or Ferguson or one of them other loopers is going to land in here with a gun and start shooting. That's how mental it has become. I'm not waiting around for that madness.'

Denzel Walsh took a long drink from the cup of coffee he'd made himself. Half an hour earlier he had been enjoying a lovely meal with his wife and a couple of friends in the new Lebanese restaurant that had just opened over on Grove Road. The owner, Ahmed Ali, was a good friend of his so the dinner and accompanying drinks were all on the house. Now here he was, being told that the only two full-time staff members he had were downing tools on him.

He cursed himself and his big mouth. Of course he didn't want to let either man go, they were the best he had, in fact they were two of the best bar staff about. His remarks had been made in the heat of the moment, the couple of Lebanese brandies putting his yapper in motion before his brain was in gear.

Catching his breath, he decided on a more conciliatory course of action.

'Look, I'm sorry lads okay? Loaf, I didn't mean what I said, I was just a bit shocked by…by all this,' he said signalling towards the blue lights outside.

'You're right, you did warn me and I should have done more. I should have asked big Andy to mind the door at the weekends. I'll speak to him tomorrow, I promise. Now can we all just take a step back here and reconsider our positions.'

'I'm sorry Denzel, I'm going,' said Loaf. 'I told you about the cousin opening a new place in the Isle of Man. He's been pestering me to come and work for him and I'm going to take him up on the offer.'

'You told me about Johnny opening a bar but you didn't tell where it was,' said the boss. 'The Isle of Man? Are you off your head? What a dump, if I won a free holiday I wouldn't go back to it. But each to their own and I'll be sorry to see you go Shaun, you're a good lad and a good barman. And you Patsy?'

'I suppose I could stay on for another week or two if it helps you out. But you'll speak to Andy, right?'

'I will, you have my word,' replied a relieved Denzel, knowing rightly that another week or two would become a month and probably another year or two, depending on Patsy's health and the bad back he was always complaining about.

Just as Loaf was about to suggest they call it a night and enjoy a staff pint together, a burly police officer came ambling through the door.

'Good evening gentleman, I'm Sergeant McElhatton,' he introduced himself.

'How's it going officer,' replied Denzel. 'What's the story out there?'

'We have a man on his way to hospital with a serious facial injury. Yet no one saw anything, not even the victim apparently. Can I ask who was working this evening, all three of you?'

'I'm the owner, I only arrived a short while ago. These two lads were working but from the conversation we've just had, they didn't see anything either.'

'That's right,' added Patsy. 'Myself and my colleague Shaun here were working but it was crazy busy so we saw nothing.'

'Nothing?'

'Not a thing.'

'And CCTV, does the bar have cameras by any chance?'

'I've been meaning to get them installed but just haven't got around to it. I'll put it on the list for next week sergeant,' said Denzel, speaking for them all with his attempts to give the police officer as little information as possible.

McElhatton knew he was on a beaten docket. If that's how the town folk wanted to play it, they could go right ahead. He had only been stationed in Ballyrush six months and he was already fed up with the tricolour-waving shithole. At this time on a Saturday night they could all shoot each other dead as far as he was concerned.

'I'm guessing then that I'm not going to get any formal statements out of you two, would that be fair to say?'

'We've nothing to tell you. I'm sorry, I wish we could be more help,' said Loaf, returning to his cleaning and deliberately running his mop over the cop's boots.

'You couldn't step back for me there please sergeant. Good man yourself.'

'Right then,' replied the officer with a deep, dissatisfied growl. 'I may need to come back tomorrow, depending on what my senior says. But if there's nothing to report then there's nothing to report.'

Lifting his hat off the bar counter and placing it back on his head, he added without smiling, 'Good night gentlemen.'

With the officer gone, the three men broke into laughter.

'A head on him like a melted wheelie bin,' scoffed Denzel. 'He didn't look one bit happy with you two lads.'

'He'll be grand,' said Loaf. 'I'm sure he knows the score by now. Whatever you say, say nothing, isn't that the County Tyrone motto?'

'Right men, I'm going to get back over to the wife. You have my permission to close the door behind me and have a pint yourselves. After you've cleaned up of course.

'And Loaf, seriously, I'm sorry about what I said earlier, it was in the heat of the moment. You've been good to me and The Barking Dog will be a lesser place without you. But life goes on I suppose. I know I probably don't deserve this but can you do me one small favour?'

'Hit me with it.'

'I've the rota done up for next week. Can you see out your shifts until I've found someone else?'

'I'll do that Denzel, no problem.'

'Thank you.' Turning to Patsy, Denzel added, 'Me and you again then Patrick, same as it ever was.'

'Same as it ever was,' replied the veteran pint puller. 'Now will you go, you're walking footprints all over the nice clean floor.'

Chapter Two

The following Friday evening Loaf Donnelly pulled his last pint in The Barking Dog.

After raising a glass with Patsy, he lifted his coat and walked out into the cool March air.

It was shortly after 6pm and traffic was heavy, particularly around the local chip shops and takeaways.

Walking through the town centre, he sat himself down for a moment on one of the newly installed benches. On it was a brass plaque that read 'Made possible by the Special EU Programmes Agency and donated to Ballyrush District Council'.

Inhaling the tempting aroma of chips that was wafting from Jerry's Diner, he looked around at how much the place had changed in the space of a few years.

Hanging baskets displaying bright flowers swung from lampposts. The front of some of the buildings had been painted over to give the impression they were occupied. The idea had attracted a bit of sniggering when it was first announced but Loaf liked it. It was colourful, a departure from the drab grey cloak that had shrouded the town for so long.

There was scaffolding up around the old Continental Cinema which had sat crumbling in silence for decades. In its heyday The Continental had attracted crowds from all over, courting couples excitedly packing into its aisles to see the new Elvis or Jimmy Dean movie. It was where in 1970 Martha Dunleavy had met Eddie Donnelly. Four years later they married before going on to have three children – Shaun, Naomi and Catherine.

The golden era of The Continental came to an abrupt halt in 1981 when the loyalist Ulster Action Force parked a car bomb outside it. Three people lost their lives in the blast, including Shaun's great-uncle Maurice who had taken a weekend job there dispensing tickets.

For over 20 years the only visitors to The Continental had been the pigeons roosting in its rafters. Now money from the European Union had set the wheels in motion towards transforming it into a 'multi-functional shared space theatre', whatever that meant.

Shaun looked at the old place and tried to imagine what it had been like in its pomp, his parents as teenagers giggling nervously as they settled in with a box of popcorn and a couple of soft drinks, his dad likely dressed in a suit and tie, his mum in her best frock and heels.

They were innocent times before the troubled times.

There was a little photograph in the hallway of his mum's house of the two of them before they were married. Martha Dunleavy had been quite the looker in her younger years. Eddie Donnelly not so much, in the picture he was thin and already starting to lose his hair, despite him only being in his early twenties.

Eddie had hit the jackpot the day his future wife had agreed to go to the pictures with him. And well did he know it.

'She was some stunner wasn't she,' his da used to laugh, proudly showing his son the black and white photo as he sat on his knee on a Saturday evening.

Frowning but secretly loving the compliment, Martha would always reply with the same: 'You've had one can too many Eddie Donnelly, that's what's wrong with you.'

Jesus how he missed his old man.

Eddie, the man responsible for the nickname Loaf, had passed away suddenly when Shaun was 22. He had just parked up the bread van that provided him with his livelihood and was settling down to his dinner when he started to complain of not feeling well.

And just like that he was gone. Sitting in his favourite armchair, Eddie Donnelly passed away.

Loaf filled his chest and exhaled a long sigh. Pulling his collar around his neck he got up from the bench and headed in the direction of The Barnacle.

There Maggie Johnston, the proprietor, greeted him with a smile and asked him how he was getting on.

'I'm doing the best Maggie. That's me finished up in The Dog this evening. Four years I was there.'

'I didn't know you were packing it in,' she replied. 'You're hardly looking for a shift are you because I could give you work in a heartbeat.'

'Thanks Maggie but I've made other plans. I'll tell you a bit more once I get this down me,' he smiled back, lifting the glass of liquid gold off the counter and taking a drink from it.

Community activists, he thought to himself after consuming half his pint in two gulps. It was another one of those terms that had crept into the Northern Ireland vocabulary.

The Good Friday Agreement. Obviously it had been a positive in that people were no longer murdering each other. But it had also thrown up some tricky questions.

Within The Agreement was the clause that prisoners on both sides of the political divide be released.

But what next? What incentive could prevent a return to the days of the bomb and bullet?

The truth was that many former prisoners had already moved away from violence of their own accord. They had used their time behind bars smartly, developing their intellectual positions by absorbing the likes of Marx and Connolly.

The politically astute men and women who came out of prison bore little resemblance to the angry young soldiers who had been dragged in years earlier.

The answer to the question 'what next' was to create paid roles as community workers or 'community activists'.

And in the main, it had worked.

In Ballyrush you had former IRA and INLA volunteers, some of whom had served long and harsh sentences at her majesty's pleasure, doing good work. They were involved in cross-community bridge building, some were running Irish language classes while others were setting up boxing clubs or creating allotments.

But it was never going to be all handshakes and happiness. The six counties were far too intricate a web of political, historical and cultural complexities for that.

There were those who hadn't signed up to The Agreement and who weren't in favour of a move away from armed struggle. More and more 'splinter groups' were emerging, factions keen to keep taking the war to the British and to each other.

Drugs, proper hard drugs, were becoming a serious problem too.

Paramilitary organisations had a lot to answer for in terms of Northern Ireland's woes. But during The Troubles they had also provided an invaluable service to local communities by keeping filth like cocaine and heroin out. Through punishment beatings or the threat of such attacks they managed to keep housing estates free of the substances that had caused so much destruction in other parts of the island, most notably Dublin where they were rife.

But following the disbandment of those paramilitary groups, crime gangs that cared nothing for political ideology had moved in.

Up until two years ago Loaf Donnelly had never set eyes on a bag of cocaine. Then one day it was offered to him as he served a group of young men who had called in for a drink before heading on to Breeze, Ballyrush's only nightclub.

Cocaine was what Mickey Kinneally and Frankie Ferguson were fighting about, over which of their gangs controlled the Springdale Estate.

'It's a whole new world,' muttered Loaf to himself as he slugged down the last of his pint and held up his glass to signal to Maggie that he was ready for a refill.

Moving on to his own new world, he tuned his mind to the big adventure he was about to embark on.

His only hesitation, or rather his main hesitation, centred on his cousin, Johnny Donnelly.

Johnny was a year older than Loaf. Their fathers had started the bread delivery company together, building it into a success which at its height had ten vans on the road.

He was a stumbler, someone destined to freefall through life, picking up scrapes, bumps and bruises along the way.

Growing up, he was big in size which made him the star attraction for local bullies. And his lack of ability in the classroom meant he was never going to win a scholarship to Harvard.

A stumbler wasn't necessarily a bad thing to be. At the end of the day, not everyone was cut out for the 9-5pm grind.

Johnny's problem was his inability to think first. To give even the slightest consideration to consequence was simply beyond him.

His colourful entrepreneurial journey began after he bailed out of school at 16.

By going around local housing estates and knocking on doors, he built up a clientele of residents who wanted their lawns mowed on a regular basis. It was a fair enough job which required commitment. All was going well until he ran over the cable of his rickety old mower and almost sent himself to the big garden in the sky.

By that stage he'd had enough of pulling weeds anyway.

His next commercial leap was into the greasy world of mobile catering.

He bought himself a filthy and decrepit fish and chip van which he managed to resuscitate.

Again things were bubbling along nicely until six of his customers came down with a severe bout of food poisoning.

The incident prompted an ultimatum from the local council, either 'Donnelly's Diner' shut up shop or its owner be taken to court for breaching every health and safety regulation under the sun.

A wise man might have paused for thought after such a setback. Not JD. Within three months he was elbows deep in another industry he had neither knowledge nor experience of.

His skillset as a locksmith came from a book borrowed from the local library, of which he read the first 30 pages before convincing himself he was suitably qualified to assist people with emergency openings and repairs.

He was not suitably qualified.

When the arse fell out of 'Donnelly's Door Solutions' he decided he would make a fine pest control officer.

Each failed venture brought with it bother of some form or another. But it was his car wash that took his troubles to a whole new level.

Initially 'Donnelly's Deluxe Drive-Thru' did a roaring trade with its soap and shine the talk of Ballyrush.

Then one evening it was pointed out to Johnny that about 75 per-cent of his customers were young men and women who might be interested in purchasing these new party pills everyone was popping.

Suddenly Purvis Street was one long tailback of noisy Novas and Sierras, none of them in need of a wash.

It took the local cops about five minutes to work out what was going on. A search of the premises turned up £10,000 of ecstasy tablets, a stash that landed Johnny on the front page of the Ballyrush Herald, much to his parents' fury.

He eventually beat the charge, his solicitor arguing that anyone could have planted the pills in the unit his client used as his headquarters.

But his card was marked and arrests for drink driving, urinating in public and disorderly behaviour quickly followed.

The announcement then that he was moving away, going to start afresh on the Isle of Man, was greeted with little opposition from within the Donnelly clan.

From Loaf's point of view, Johnny was what the great philosophers of Ancient Greece might have classed as 'a bit of a bollocks'. But it was also hard not to be drawn in by his impulsive, reckless, ridiculous approach to life.

The phone call was completely out of the blue. But it was pure Johnny Donnelly.

'Yes lad it's me, your number one cousin. What are you doing with yourself these days?'

'Same as always, scraping a living working in The Barking Dog. What about you?'

'I've moved over here to the Isle of Man. I'm planning on taking over a bar.'

'You running a bar? Johnny you've never even worked in a pub never mind run one.'

'I've been thrown out of plenty though. But here, I didn't know anything about running a mobile chip van either and look how that turned out.'

'It turned out to be a disaster. A woman ended up in hospital.'

'Exactly. Now what about this, you come over and be my head barman. You've worked in these places, you can pour ale as well as any man I've ever seen.'

Loaf had never been particularly ambitious. He had been pulling pints for years and was content with it as long as his pay packet was waiting for him on a Sunday evening.

But head barman? He liked the sound of it.

'I don't even know where the Isle of Man is Johnny.'

'It's a half an hour flight from Belfast. Will you think about it for me? I really want to give this a go but I can't do it on my own. Come on cuz, it'll be great craic. You'll love it over here, the bar is right on the seafront. Imagine it - me, you, a few cold beers, a couple of nice Manx birds to keep us company. I'll set you up with accommodation and everything.'

'Okay, give me a few weeks to think about it. And you'll have somewhere for me to stay, is that right?'

'I guarantee it.'

'It does sound tempting. I'll be in touch Johnny, I promise.'

'Good lad, we'll chat soon.'

Following the conversation, Loaf had visited the local library where he borrowed a book titled 'The Isle of Man – A Jewel in the Irish Sea'.

The book was packed with pictures of smiling holidaymakers enjoying themselves on horse drawn trams or sunning themselves on the beach that necklaced the island's capital, Douglas.

It did look extremely inviting, more so when Loaf was able to ascertain that the locals spoke English and the main currency was sterling. On a page listing interesting facts he learned that disco trio The Bee Gees were born on the island and that Formula One driver Nigel Mansell had once been a police officer there.

Relaxed in the cosy surrounds of The Barnacle, he decided he was doing the right thing. After all, what was the worst that could happen? If it didn't work out or if Johnny let him down as well he might, he could simply turn around and come home again.

Fortune favours the brave, isn't that what they say, he told himself as he sipped his pint.

His only other concern was his mum. Since his father's death, it had been just the two of them at home.

His youngest sister, Naomi, was away at university in Aberdeen. She came home every three months but when she did she tended to spend most of her time partying with her pals.

His other sister, Catherine, life had pulled her in a very different direction.

She was shacked up with Ricky Woods, a local scumbag and druggie. They lived in a small flat over in Wallace Heights where Catherine was doing her best to bring up their two children, Dana and Michael.

Invariably her husband was drunk or in prison. Loaf had lost count of the number of times he had confronted Woods, warning him to either get his act together or to leave his sister alone. The response was always the same, his brother-in-law breaking down in tears like the snivelling weasel he was and vowing to do better.

He never did do better and the big wheel kept on turning – Woods making Catherine's life a misery and her relying on their mum for support and more often than not, for money.

What would become of his mum if he wasn't around for their morning cup of tea or at night when she stayed awake to make sure he locked the front door when he came in after his shift?

A knot formed in his chest as he thought about it, his dreamy notions of sunny days in the Isle of Man suddenly starting to cloud over.

Chapter Three

He needn't have worried about telling his mum.

She was as excited as he was, even revealing a story that he had never heard before.

Helping him pack the suitcase that they had hauled out of the hot press, she told him, 'Me and your dad spent a weekend there one time. It was before any of you three came along.'

As she expertly folded shirts and t-shirts, Martha recalled with an obvious fondness their few days together on the island.

'We walked for miles and miles, the sun shining down on us. I remember your father picking a red flower and putting it in my hair.

'There we were, the two of us laying on the beach at Ramsey, listening to Radio Caroline on a little transistor radio he had. Me with my flower in my hair, your father with his shirt unbuttoned thinking he was so cool.

'He was a real romantic you know,' she added with a melancholy smile.

Returning to the task at hand, she held up a pair of faded boxer shorts that had Fred Flintstone on one side and Barney Rubble on the other. Emblazoned across the arse was the word 'Yabbadabbadoo!'.

'Shaun Donnelly if you think you are leaving this house with these in your suitcase then you have another thing coming.'

'Mum, those are my lucky boxers.'

'Lucky? I've seen some of the women you've brought home son. If you think these boxers have brought you luck then you need your head examined.'

'Well that's not a very nice thing to say. What about Evelyn, you liked Evelyn.'

'I liked Evelyn very much. But what about that last one you were with, the one with the screeching laugh? I could have strangled you the night you landed in here with her. God love her, a tsunami wouldn't have taken her.'

'What's a man to do, I was drunk and the craic was good. Anyway, back to The Flintstones. All in favour, raise their hand.'

Looking around the room at the imaginary jury Martha announced, 'All the votes have been counted and it looks like it's one for and one against. And as the bill payer I get the deciding vote. Bye Fred, bye Barney,' she added, gleefully flinging the shorts into the hall, from where they would be transported to their final destination – the bin.

Surrendering to his mother's better judgement, Loaf rattled on about The Barking Dog and some of the characters who frequented the place.

Only half tuned in to what he was saying, Martha looked at him and thought how it would do him good to get away for a while. He didn't like to talk about it but his father's death had hit him hard. A change of scenery would do him no harm at all. He was a good boy, a good son. He'd never once brought the police to her door, which was more than a lot of mothers in Ballyrush could say.

She would miss him and his antics – the late night staggers in the door having stayed on for more than a pint after work, the requests to iron his favourite shirt because she was 'the best ironer in the world'.

There was another reason she was glad he was going, one that she was keeping to herself because it felt a little bit selfish. But with her son gone, there would be two spare rooms. She secretly hoped she might be able to entice Catherine to move home with the kids, away from her no-good partner.

Catherine could have Shaun's old room while she could buy a set of bunk beds for Dana and Michael. No more nights waiting for a phone call from her daughter telling her that Ricky Woods had wrecked the flat again or that he'd been arrested and she needed to borrow money to bail him out. No more dreading every knock at the door.

It was her plan, a mother's plan.

The only thing niggling at her about her son's going away was Johnny Donnelly.

'He had his mother's heart broke,' she said. 'I had her on the phone a few nights, her crying her eyes out. Just you look out for yourself son and you know where we are if anything goes wrong.'

'I'll be grand mum. I'm a big boy now you know,' he replied with a reassuring smile.

'I know. But a mother never stops worrying. It's our cross to bear in life. Now, what about a cup of tea? We're nearly sorted here.'

ON the advice of the local travel agent, he decided to take the ferry rather than flying.

Going by plane would cost him over £100. Travelling by sea would be cheaper and less complicated, the lady at Easy Holidays had informed him.

On the Saturday he was due to depart, his mum insisted on accompanying him to the bus station.

'You have your ticket?'

'For the thousandth time mum, yes I have my ticket.'

'And you have your sea sickness tablets?'

'What tablets? I thought I was supposed to take them all at the same time so I downed the lot this morning.'

'Listen here Shaun Donnelly, you may be six foot but you're not too tall for a slap from your mother.'

Both of them laughing, he asked, 'You'll be okay mum won't you? You won't be lonely without me?'

'I'll be fine son. Sure I'm at the bingo three nights a week aren't I? And then I've my bowls on a Friday and Saturday night down at the cricket club. With you gone I might even start asking Artie Maxwell over for a drink.'

'Artie Maxwell? Was he not done for flashing at the old ladies outside Woolworths?'

'No, that was his brother Barney. Artie's the one who wears the trilby all the time, looks dead smart.'

'Whatever floats your boat mum. Just don't be getting yourself into any trouble.'

'If I can find trouble at my age I'll be getting into it, don't you worry about that.'

It was just after 9am when the big red bus trundled into Ballyrush station. As the driver stepped down to open the luggage hatch, Loaf gave his mum a hug.

'I'll be back in a few months for a visit. Who knows, I could be back next week, depending on this cousin of mine. And I'll call you. You've charged that mobile phone I bought you, haven't you?'

'I have although I haven't a clue how to work the bloody thing. But I'll sit down this evening and see if I can figure it out.'

'Do because I'll be calling you on it.'

As he stepped up on to the bus, his mum called after him.

'Shaun, whatever you do, enjoy yourself. Get as much of that sea air into you as you can.'

'I will mum, I promise. Take care.'

Martha waved as the coach set off towards Belfast, her son waving back at her.

As they left the station it suddenly dawned on him that this was it, he was on his own.

Nerves mingled with adrenalin as he searched his backpack for the Mars Bar and bottle of water he'd brought for the journey.

WHEN he awoke from his doze the bus was turning down into Belfast Port.

Wiping the sleep from his eyes, he caught his first glimpse of the Seacat, a huge white ship with the famous Three Legs of Man on its side.

Ahead of him was a three and a half hour journey across the Irish Sea. He wondered how he was going to kill the time.

Dragging his suitcase behind him, he joined the queue for security. On reaching the front he was greeted with a smile by a pretty attendant who glanced at his passport and told him to enjoy his trip.

He gulped down a deep breath of ocean air before navigating the gangway that took him on to the ferry.

The short walk led to a large open plan room which was already a cacophony of noise.

The place was buzzing with the sound of excited children, anxious parents and a hen party of about 25 women, all half-drunk by the look of them. At the heart of the gang was the bride-to-be who was wearing a veil and carrying an inflatable, naked man under her arm. On the table in front of them was a garish bottle of green spirits which they were preparing to demolish. A woman wearing a pink t-shirt with the words 'Sheila's Shaggers' on it was handing out plastic shot glasses while her fellow party animals broke into an impromptu sing song of 'Proud Mary'.

Trying not to get overwhelmed by the colourful canvas that was unfolding before his eyes, Loaf looked at his watch. It was 11.45am.

Making his way into the centre of the room, he took up position against a pillar and began to get his bearings.

Circular windows dotted both sides of the lounge so passengers could look out on to the sea.

Signs revealed that in neighbouring rooms there was a bar, a café and a retail area.

Sitting himself down, he unzipped his suitcase and had a riffle through his clothes and the various other bits and pieces he had packed. Among them was a handful of his favourites CDs – Bagatelle Gold, Bruce Springsteen's Greatest Hits and If I Should Fall From Grace With God by The Pogues.

Once he was satisfied that everything was fine and that he could safely leave his belongings without fear of them being nicked – where would a would-be thief go with them? – he decided to have a roam around.

Moving into the next room he found himself in an arcade, a room lined with video games and fruit and poker machines.

Poker machines were a bad habit he had picked up while working in the bar and it was a rare day when he would walk past one without having a go.

Pulling two pound coins from his pocket he dropped them into the slot and hit the deal button. To his delight up came four nines, netting him a tidy £8. The gambling card was a two, prompting him to go higher.

In the space of about three minutes he had turned his £2 into £16 and he was thrilled to hear the coins falling into the tray below.

It was a good omen, he felt, as he pocketed his winnings and moved on through the ferry.

He stopped at the café and bought himself a tuna and coleslaw sandwich. To wash it down he purchased a pint of Carlsberg which was served to him in a plastic beaker. Glasses probably weren't a good idea on board a craft that tended to lurch this way and that depending on the tides, he thought to himself.

Returning to his seat, he tucked into his early lunch and watched as the hen party embarked on a conga line. A skinny steward approached them to ask them to settle down. But he ended up being pulled into the cackling carnival.

Loaf laughed to himself as the staff member tried to wriggle from their clutches only to be dragged back in for one final lap.

Having finished his meal he decided to take a walk out on deck.

He had to push hard to open the door as the cold wind whipped against it. Outside, the sea mist hit him a welcome smack.

There was little to see other than a seemingly endless sheet of white-tipped waves. But it was bracing and again he breathed deeply, filling himself with salty air.

'You going over to work,' asked a voice from behind him.

Turning on his heel at the unexpected question he was met by a friendly face, a Black guy smoking a cigarette.

'I am actually. My cousin has just taken over a pub in Douglas and he has appointed me his head barman.'

'Ah, nice one,' said the London accent. 'It's pretty hectic over there right now.'

'Why's that?'

'They're building a new hospital so the island is mobbed with brickies, scaffolders, joiners, labourers. It's costing something like £100 million, a proper big job that's going to take a couple of years.'

'Excellent,' said Loaf, delighted to learn that the pub was going to be busy.

'I'm Terry,' said the muscular stranger, offering his hand which was hard and leathery to the touch.

'I'm Shaun but everyone calls me Loaf. My dad was a breadman you see.'

'Loaf? I like that,' laughed Terry. What's the name of the pub you're going to be working in?'

'You know this Terry, I'm not even sure. Johnny, the cousin, will have all those details. He's meeting me at the sea terminal.'

'Fair enough. Maybe we'll bump into each other again, I do try and get into town for a pint now and again.'

After parting company with Terry, Loaf returned to his seat and fished out a book of wordsearches his mother had packed for him.

Before he knew it, three hours had passed.

Getting up to stretch his legs, he decided on one final stroll along the deck.

Outside he met Terry again, this time with a friend, both of them smoking and chatting.

'And there she is, the good old Isle of Man,' said Terry, pointing off to his right.

Sure enough there it was rising up out of the sea, bathed in a watery sunshine.

'Two years I've lived there now,' revealed Terry. 'It's a nice place but it's a nice place to leave too. It tends to get claustrophobic.

'Right Mr Loaf, I'll be seeing you. And good luck with the new job,' he added as he headed off to collect his things.

Thirty minutes later and the ferry was docked, its passengers ready to disembark.

Stepping off the steel walkway that took him from sea to land, Loaf Donnelly put his two feet on Manx soil for the first time.

Chapter Four

He made his way through the sea terminal via a long carpeted corridor.

Rounding a corner he was met with a shout of 'There he is, my new head barman.'

Looking in the direction of the voice, he spotted his cousin stepping out of the crowd that had congregated to greet loved ones.

He had changed, thought Loaf at first glance. He was even heavier than before and he looked tired. He was losing his hair too.

But he was definitely Johnny Donnelly.

'Yes wee cousin, it's great to see you. How was the crossing,' Johnny asked, stepping in to give him a hug.

'It was nice actually, more comfortable than I was expecting. How are you Johnny?'

It was overcast as they began their walk and there was a biting breeze blowing in off the water.

For someone who had never seen it before, it was a lot to take in.

Loch Promenade or 'the prom' as Johnny referred to it, stretched in the shape of a croissant for about a mile around Douglas seafront, looking down on to a stony, seaweed-strewn beach.

The buildings were mostly Victorian-era guesthouses and hotels, many of them in need of freshening up after another winter of salty gales and unforgiving showers.

Loaf zipped his coat up as they headed towards The Thirsty Sailor, the bar Johnny had decided to take on.

His cousin chatted away, filling him in on island life and his plans for the future. But Loaf was elsewhere, hypnotised.

He noted the public gardens as they passed them, thinking it would be a lovely place to sit in the summertime.

The stone tower with the flag atop it a little way out to sea. The Sugarland Hotel, The Four Winds, The Ellan Vannin, The Bay Lodge – he was lost in it all.

Snapping himself back to reality, he noted that Johnny was now several feet in front of him and still babbling away.

'Johnny, slow down will you. I've this suitcase with me and you're sprinting on like Linford Christie.'

'Sorry buddy, it's just that it's so bloody cold and I'm gasping for a coffee.'

Suddenly a coffee seemed like the greatest idea in the world. Loaf duly picked up the pace. He also realised that he was ravenous with hunger.

'I'm going to need to eat shortly, I've had nothing today other than a sandwich on the boat.'

'Don't worry, I have it covered. Come on, it's not far now,' his cousin assured him as they continued their march.

Passing The Villa Marina which appeared to be a large grassy area with an adjoining theatre, Johnny announced grandly, 'And there it is, The Thirsty Sailor.'

Loaf's eyes nearly fell out of his head when he saw what was in front of him.

The Thirsty Sailor was a boarded up building that looked like it had been out business for years. The letters spelling out the pub's name were all gone apart from the 'STY' in Thirsty.

'What do you think,' Johnny declared proudly, either oblivious to or ignoring Mother Nature's dark humour.

Loaf's immediate reaction was to tell him it was a shit hole and that he was furious he hadn't mentioned the pub was a rundown kip.

But looking at his cousin, grinning with his arm outstretched as if he had just unveiled the world's first time machine, he decided instead to be kind.

'It…it has potential I suppose,' he said.

Seeing the grimace, Johnny quickly moved to alleviate his fears.

'I know it doesn't look like much but wait until you see the inside.'

Due to the pile of letters and junk mail that had accumulated behind it, Johnny had to use his shoulder to get the front door open.

But once inside, Loaf's heart lifted.

It was perfect. Yes it was dusty and a little grimy but it was practically intact.

The roof was high and the bar counter solid oak. There were six brass beer pumps in need of a good polish but which otherwise appeared to be in full working order.

There was a pool table with a complete set of balls and a couple of cues.

He explored the place slowly, checking each appliance like a doctor giving a patient an MOT.

The more he saw, the more impressed he was. The fridges, the optics, the glasswasher, the ice machine, they were all there, frozen in time. It was almost like the previous owner had pulled the door closed one day and just never returned.

As he surveyed the décor and the pictures on the wall, he began to notice a motorcycle theme.

Seeing him staring up at a photo of Joey Dunlop, Johnny, now armed with two steaming mugs of coffee, informed him, 'They love all that motorbike stuff over here. It's like a religion to them. If I've learnt anything since arriving on this island it's that Manx people love motorcycles and they love being Manx.'

'Johnny, this is great,' said Loaf, capping his inspection with one final 360 degree turn.

'Isn't it? Oh ye of little faith, you think I didn't see your face out there? Come me with a second,' he instructed, heading back out the front door.

'You're on Broadway baby,' Johnny laughed, pointing down at a sign which confirmed that The Thirsty Sailor was indeed on Broadway. 'And on Broadway, magic happens. It's rough looking now but a bit of elbow grease will soon sort it out. What do you reckon?'

'I think you've hit the jackpot here JD.'

'That's what I like to hear. I've already spoken to the brewery about stock and they said to give them a call when we're ready to open.'

Back inside, Loaf placed his half-empty cup on one of the tables.

'Johnny, can I ask you something. Where are you getting the money for this? I don't remember you being a millionaire back home. Running a pub isn't cheap. There's rent to cover, you have rates, VAT, there's staff to pay, stock, electricity, heating, maintenance. It's an expensive game.'

Looking at him with a shake of his head and an expression of faux disappointment, his cousin told him, 'You've always been a worrier Shaun. Serious Shaun, that's what they should call you. Don't you be stressing about where I'm getting the money, that's for me to take care of.'

Quickly changing the subject, Johnny added, 'Now what about food? There's a steakhouse a couple of doors up and it does the best grub in Douglas. Let's go and see if Antonio is open yet. After that I'll take you up to your digs.'

Over a couple of monster T-bones with all the trimmings they chatted about family. Loaf updated him on his sisters, in particular Catherine and how she was still mixed up with the disaster that was Ricky Woods.

Johnny talked about his brother Mark who had come out as gay the day after his 21st birthday.

'Mum was fine with it but my da struggled. He's fine now but it was a bit of a shock at the start. I couldn't care less, whatever gets you through the day, that's the way I look at it.'

By the time they were finished eating Loaf was absolutely stuffed. Leaning back in his seat he rubbed his stomach and announced, 'I could lay down and sleep.'

'It's been a long day for you with all the travelling. What do you want to do, walk up to your flat or I can drive us up in the van. It's about 20 minutes by foot.'

'We'll walk, it'll give me a chance to shake off some of this dinner.'

'Fair enough. Let me pay for this, I'll grab a quick piss and we'll be on our way,' Johnny insisted.

Evening was closing in as they strolled up through Derby Square.

'So here's the deal. I've got you a wee one bedroom place on Westfield Terrace. I've had a look at it and it's fine. I've put down a month's rent so you don't have to worry about that.

'We'll start into the pub tomorrow with a view to having it open a week from Friday. As my top dog I'll pay you £10 an hour and you can work as many hours as you want. I already have a few young people lined up to help us with the clean-up. Hopefully we'll have four or five staff on the books by the time we go live.

'How does all that sound?'

'That all sounds pretty good to me. I was only on £7.50 an hour in The Barking Dog so it's a step up from that.'

'Excellent. And as head barman, you can make most of the decisions. Things like entertainment, promotions, hiring and firing, you know more about that stuff than I do so I'll leave it all with you.'

Loaf was suddenly nervous. He'd never had to carry such responsibility before. He decided though that he was up for the challenge.

'No problem, there's nothing there that I can't handle,' he told his cousin and himself at the same time.

By the time they turned on to Westfield Terrace he was feeling really weary, his suitcase starting to weigh him down like it was full of lead.

Westfield Terrace was a cul de sac consisting of about a dozen four-storey houses. He was staying in number 12 which had been broken up into four flats.

The property was tucked away in the corner with a long hedge running down the side of it. What lay beyond the hedge he couldn't tell due to the rapidly fading light.

'Here you are, home sweet home,' said his cousin, handing him a key with 'Apt 3' written on it.

'Are you not coming up,' asked Loaf, seeing Johnny preparing to head off again.

'You don't need me to hold your hand do you? You go in the door, up to the third floor and that's you. I put some food in the fridge yesterday so you'll have the makings of a breakfast at least.

'I'll be in the bar from 9am tomorrow. Come down and meet me when you're up and about.'

'Okay, thanks,' called Loaf as his cousin began to walk away.

Alone, he crossed the road to get a better look at the house. There was a light in the top window but apart from that, it appeared to be empty.

As he prepared to go up the front steps, a rustling in the hedge broke the quiet.

It startled him. But not nearly as much as what happened next.

'Who are you,' asked a male voice.

The unexpected question almost caused him to pee in his pants right there on the spot.

He looked in the direction it had come from but couldn't see a thing.

Absolutely terrified, he stammered, 'Hello is…is there somebody there?'

The leaves swished again, followed by the same question - 'Who are you?'

The voice was inquisitive rather than sinister. In different circumstances it could have been wholly humorous.

Loaf was exhausted and in no form for shocks like this. Rather than hang about, he took the steps two at a time and stuck the key in the door as quickly as he could. Slamming it behind him, he found himself in a hallway. There was a welcome silence as he stopped to catch his breath.

After a couple of minutes of gathering himself together he decided to venture up the stairs. The light was on a timer so at every floor he had to press a button to make sure he wasn't left clambering about in the dark.

Eventually he found himself outside flat number three.

The green door opened up on to a combined living and kitchen area which had recently been done up. The place was furnished, including a television set in the corner. To the right was the bedroom which had a window that looked out on to a rear laneway.

Plonking himself down in an armchair, he tried to take stock of what had just happened.

Whose voice was it? And why did they want to know who he was?

As he sat there he was gripped again by an enormous tiredness.

He wanted to get acquainted with his new abode, to have a poke around and see how things like the shower worked.

Half an hour. I'll get up in half an hour he vowed as he crawled under the duvet on the bed.

Within two minutes he was gone, deep in slumber, his last conscious thought taking him back to the noisy hen party from earlier.

'I wonder how Sheila's Shaggers are getting on,' he asked himself dreamily before dropping off into a ten hour coma.

Chapter Five

Loaf woke the next day shortly after 7am feeling like he could conquer the world.

It was as if he had crammed a week's sleep into a single night. With the sun streaming in the window he bounced out of bed, into the kitchen and knocked on the kettle for a cup of tea.

It didn't take long to get to know the place. The cupboards were predictable - crockery, saucepans, a deep fat fryer in need of cleaning.

In the fridge he found sausages and bacon which he happily dispatched into the frying pan.

'Thank you Johnny boy,' he announced loudly to himself.

While breakfast was gently sizzling he decided to tackle the shower. It couldn't have been much simpler – pull the cord, turn the knob, enjoy.

As he stood there savouring the warm droplets he snorted in derisive laughter at the previous evening's events.

Clearly he had been hallucinating, tiredness causing his mind to play tricks on him.

Voices in hedges. You're losing the plot Donnelly, he thought as he dried himself off.

From his suitcase he fetched the little radio he had brought across with him.

He twiddled with the tuning dial until he found a station that revealed itself to be Manx Gold. The DJ was talking about his 'mystery sound', a competition Loaf had always detested due to the randomness of the answers. He remembered listening to the same muck for weeks and weeks on a station back home only for the presenter to eventually reveal the 'mystery sound' was him lighting a fag using the cigarette lighter in his 1986 Ford Taurus.

How was anyone supposed to guess that?

'Ya fuckin' prick,' was Loaf's irate response on hearing the impossibly obscure solution.

Mug of tea in hand, he opened one of the two front windows and had a look out.

From his heightened vantage point he was able to see what was on the other side of the hedge. It was a large garden in which was embedded a sign that read 'Sunny View Care Home'.

A bloody care home? Maybe it was the ghost of a past resident who had called out to him he joked, now even more confident that the incident had been a figment of his depleted imagination.

By the time he was fed and dressed it was just after 8.30am. He wanted to be at the bar for 9am. Johnny was his cousin and was hardly going to dock his wages but punctuality was important to him. He had a real problem with people who said they would be somewhere at such and such a time only to rock up 30 minutes late as if it was okay.

His next challenge was going to be finding his way to The Thirsty Sailor. It had been easy the night before when it was a case of follow the leader. This morning the task was a whole lot more daunting. He remembered two landmarks that might help him – The Castle Tavern and Derby Square. Find those two and he wouldn't be far off the mark.

It was a cleaning day so jeans, t-shirt and a hoodie were the chosen uniform.

A quick rinse of the dishes and he was ready to head out. But just as he was about to leave he heard the front door of the flat above him shut.

Keen to see who else was living in the property, he waited until they were halfway down the stairs before he stepped out.

Making a pretend fuss about locking his door, he looked up to see an attractive young woman coming towards him. She had curly black hair and was dressed in black jeans, trainers and a green waterproof jacket.

As she passed him she smiled and said 'hi' in an accent that was neither English nor Irish.

American perhaps, he wondered as he followed her down, keeping his distance so as not to come across as creepy.

Outside, he stopped for a moment. Firstly to let his very lovely housemate go on and secondly so he could retrace last night's happenings.

Returning to where he was when he heard 'the voice', he looked up at the house and then at the hedge.

It was the oddest thing, he remarked as he headed off into town.

Loaf had only gone a short way when he spotted The Castle Tavern. As he passed it he made a mental note of other nearby street names that would help him navigate his way home should he take a wrong turn at some point.

It was nippy but nice as he strolled Douglas's residential streets. The sun was in the sky but nowhere near full throttle. The year was still only a pup.

Making his way on to Derby Square, he congratulated himself on finding his bearings so quickly.

Turning on to Broadway he stopped momentarily to get a look around him. An unremarkable mish mash of guesthouses and small businesses, it bore absolutely no resemblance to its glitzy New York namesake. To the point where he wondered if it had been named after Broadway in South Belfast rather than the star-studded USA thoroughfare.

Looking at his watch, it was 8.59am. Perfect timing.

The door to the pub was open and Johnny was just taking his coat off.

'Good morning cousin. How did you get on in the flat? Did you sleep?'

'I slept like a dead man,' replied Loaf, giving the place another look over. 'And thanks for the food, I had a lovely breakfast.'

'No bother at all. So here's the plan, this place needs cleaned from top to bottom. I have another couple of staff coming in shortly to help out so don't you be killing yourself, get them to do the bulk of the work. Get them to lift all this litter,' he said, pointing to the mess of letters, fliers and menus. 'The walls all need washed down, the floors need scrubbed and the toilets need a good going over.'

The toilets were something Loaf hadn't examined yet. Following a sign that read 'WC', he found himself at the top of a steep set of steps.

'The toilets are downstairs,' he noted with a frown.

'You'll find that in a lot of pubs around here. I think it's something to do with the plumbing,' Johnny explained.

Venturing down, he first checked the men's room and then the women's. One of the urinals in the men's was cracked and in need of replacing.

In both bathrooms he tried the taps and flushed the toilets. There was a smell of sewers and stale water but nothing that couldn't be rectified with a couple of bottles of bleach and Toilet Duck.

'Somebody gets a few drinks in them, they could take a nasty tumble down there,' Loaf said to his cousin as he walked back up the tiled steps while holding on to the rail.

'The thought had crossed my mind too. But what can we do? We'll worry about it when the time comes. Now, first things first, let's get these boards down off these windows and let some light in here.'

With the Irish Sea as their witness, the two cousins began the task of removing the heavy wooden panels. First one, then the next until they were all gone.

Like Lazarus emerging from his tomb, The Thirsty Sailor slowly stood up, rubbed its eyes and came back to life.

It needed work, there was no getting away from it. Two of the window panes were beyond saving and the upholstery was tired and torn in places.

But it was functional, that was the main thing. It wasn't like there was water running down the walls or vermin scurrying about the floor.

It was solid and it had heaps of character.

'When I'm out today I'll arrange to have the seats recovered and I'll speak to someone about new windows. One of the urinals downstairs is broken as well so I'll get a plumber in to have a look at it. That's an upholsterer, a glazer and a plumber. What else – a butcher, a baker, a candlestick maker,' laughed Johnny.

Loaf laughed as well but wondered again who was bankrolling things. The Johnny Donnelly he knew had never stayed in the one place long enough to afford all this.

His concerns were broken by a loud knock on the front door which was already open.

'Michael, good morning. Come in,' called Johnny on seeing a tall thin lad with a shock of ginger hair tentatively making his way inside.

'You're very welcome to The Thirsty Sailor Michael. This is my cousin Shaun but everyone calls him Loaf. He's going to be your boss.'

As Loaf shook Michael's hand the front door opened again. This time it was someone he recognised and was very happy to see for the second time in as many hours.

'And Abbey, thank you for joining us Abbey,' said Johnny in a voice that suggested it wasn't their first time to meet.

'Hey Johnny, how are things? So this is the place you were telling me about. Not bad, not bad at all,' she said, taking a look around her.

Turning her attention to the other people in the room, her eyes rested on Loaf until the Rolodex in her brain reminded her who he was.

'Mr Apartment Number Three.'

'That's me. I'm Shaun but everyone calls me Loaf.'

'Loaf?'

'My dad was a breadman. It was a name I picked up in school and it's stuck with me ever since.'

'I see…' said Abbey.

'Loaf and I are cousins,' Johnny told her. 'He's worked in pubs for years and knows everything there is to know about them. He's going to be my head honcho.'

'I see…' said Abbey for a second time. 'So should we call you Shaun or Loaf? Or Mr Loaf? Or boss,' she asked with a cheeky smile.

'Loaf will do the best,' he said, his face reddening with embarrassment.

'Fair enough. It's very nice to meet you Loaf. I'm Abbey Vincent all the way from the city of Saint John in Canada.'

Okay,' said Johnny with a clap of his hands that said he was keen to get things moving. 'We have Loaf, we have Abbey and we have Michael. Michael meet Abbey, Abbey this is Michael. Are we going to stand around all day saying each other's names? No we are not, we are going to get this place looking like a proper bar.'

Loaf took control, allocating the job of cleaning the walls, window frames and sills to Michael.

Abbey was given the floor to look after. It was an even more arduous task, one that would require a toothbrush to lift the dirt out from between the tiles.

It was a marathon not a sprint, Loaf assured them. Anything that didn't get done today could be finished tomorrow.

Impressed by his cousin's leadership skills, Johnny stood and watched for about ten minutes before announcing that he had to go out.

'I'll make a few calls, see if I can locate those tradesmen we talked about earlier.'

Lifting the van keys off the bar, he called as he headed out the door, 'Keep up the good work team.'

By 1pm everyone had worked up an appetite. Loaf declared lunch, to which Michael replied that he knew a decent sandwich shop nearby.

'Sounds good. Here's £20, I'll get it back off Johnny when I see him. Get me tuna, mayo and coleslaw on brown bread. Abbey?'

'Brown bread for me too. I'll have chicken, mayo with loads of salad. And a Sprite please.'

'I'll be as quick as I can,' said Michael, sauntering off at a pace that suggested he had no intention of being as quick as he could.

Loaf put on the kettle and asked Abbey if she would like tea or coffee.

'I'll have a coffee please, straight black. So tell me Shaun, how long have you been in the Isle of Man?'

Looking at his watch he said, 'Ummm, about 18 hours.'

'That long? You should apply for citizenship,' she replied with a laugh. 'Seriously, you only arrived yesterday?'

'Yip, I'm fresh off the boat.'

'Well I hope you have a great time. I've been here six months and I've loved it. Unfortunately I've only two weeks left before I have to go back to Canada.'

'That's not so good,' said Loaf, genuinely disappointed that they wouldn't be working together.

'I know. But all good parties come to an end eventually.'

'How do you know Johnny then,' he asked her.

'He comes in the odd time to Blake's Bar where I work down on the quay. He was telling me about taking this place over and said there would be a couple of weeks' work if I wanted it. There's going to be a massive credit card bill waiting for me when I get home so I said yes.'

Abbey was a law student at Saint John University. She was about to begin her final year when, much to her parents' chagrin, she decided to take a breather and go travelling.

Her first stop had been Liverpool where she had crashed on a friend's sofa. She quickly found work in the world famous Cavern Club before the Isle of Man came on her radar.

They chatted until Michael returned with lunch. As they ate he revealed he was 19 and a Manxie, born and bred. He was studying sports psychology at the local college, the plan being to one day move to Australia.

Loaf told him how he had just arrived and Abbey explained that she was preparing to leave.

Fed and watered, they returned to their respective chores. By the time they looked up again, it was 5pm.

'I think we'll call it a day at that,' announced Loaf. 'I don't know about you two but I'm beat.'

'Beat,' inquired Abbey. 'Beat? Don't talk to me about being tired. I'm starting a shift in Blake's at 6pm.'

'And I'm going to Underworld tonight with my mates,' said Michael. 'We're meeting for pints at 7pm and then on to the club at 11pm. Party on.'

Loaf looked at the two of them, worried that neither of them would show the following morning.

'It's a 9am start tomorrow. Please tell me you'll both be here because I can't do this on my own.'

'I'll be here,' said Abbey. 'I need the money, remember?'

'I'll be here too. As long as I'm in bed for 3am, I'll be fine,' added Michael.

'Cool. Right, I'll see you both in the morning then.'

'Why don't you come to Blake's for a drink? It'll be quiet until about 9pm, you can keep me company,' asked Abbey.

It was an unexpected and very tempting offer. But he hadn't unpacked properly yet and he needed to go food shopping.

'The next night, I promise. I've a few things to do this evening, that's all.'

'Okay, but I'm holding you to that,' she said as they pulled on their coats and prepared to leave.

Just as they were walking out the door, Johnny returned to lock up. Loaf gave him a brief rundown of the day's developments along with a vow that they would all be back in the morning.

Outside Loaf watched Abbey as she walked away, the temptation to go and sit with her in Blake's still buzzing in his ear.

A quick sniff of the t-shirt he was wearing told him all he needed to know.

A visit to the little supermarket he had passed on his way to work followed by a shower and an early night was the sensible play.

He had plenty of thoughts to keep him company as he trekked back up through Derby Square.

Outside number 12 Westfield Terrace he placed his shopping bags on the ground to get his keys out of his pocket.

As he did so he heard it again.

'Who are you?'

Chapter Six

He was about 80 years old and wearing a flat cap. He had a thin moustache that turned up at the ends.

Loaf eyed him with frustration.

'It was you. You're the one who's been lurking about here asking me who I am.'

'That's correct,' replied flat cap. 'Are you going to tell me?'

'Why should I, it's none of your business.'

'It is my business, I'm the chief constable of this island.'

'Show me your badge then.'

'It's inside, in my office.'

'Lies. You're not the chief constable, you're just an old coot who looks over hedges and annoys people. Now go away, I'm too tired to be standing here arguing with you.'

Loaf gathered his shopping and started up the steps when flat cap spoke again.

'I'm…I'm Magnus Quayle,' he called.

With a sigh of reluctance, Loaf put his shopping down on the doorstep and turned back around.

His former heckler cut a lonely figure in the day's dying embers.

'Well Magnus Quayle, I'm Shaun Donnelly. Everyone calls me Loaf.'

'Hmmm, I'm not a big fan of nicknames so if you don't mind, I'll just call you Shaun,' he answered.

'What's your deal then Magnus, why are you standing about asking random strangers questions?'

'It's just something to do isn't it? Otherwise I'd be in there playing Ludo with the walking dead.'

'And you're not the chief constable, am I right?'

'Of course I'm not. I'm 84 and I live in a nursing home for crying out loud. I just make things like that up to entertain myself. The other week I saw an old one coming across your street. As she got closer I started crowing like a rooster. The nosy old cat looked over to see what was going on and I jumped up and scared the bloomers clean off her. She could be screaming yet for all I know.'

There was an elegance in his voice that became more apparent the more he spoke. Even if it was to tell a story about frightening an innocent old lady half to death.

'Well that wasn't a very charitable thing to do.'

'Oh horse whiskers. It passed the afternoon for me didn't it,' he said with a smirk.

Loaf smirked back.

From the breast pocket of the jacket he was wearing, Magnus Quayle produced a cigarette box. He withdrew from it a cigarillo, the same kind Loaf's great-uncle Maurice used to smoke.

'Do you want one,' he asked, offering the case over the hedge.

'I don't. But thank you,' Loaf declined as a fine plume of smoke curled away in the April air.

'Magnus I'm going to have to get it in here but it's been nice meeting you.'

'It's been nice meeting you too Mr Shaun Donnelly. Maybe we'll chat again?'

'Well I'm living here now so there's a good chance our paths will cross soon. Good night and take care.'

THE next few days skipped by, spent in the company of Johnny, Abbey, Michael and a new crew member, Carl.

The daily routine was that everyone was on site for 9am and working by 9.15am. There was a tea break at 11am, lunch at 1pm and another 15 minute break around 3pm. At 5pm they all finished up for the day.

They were a good team, everyone mucking in, doing their fair share and having a good time. Johnny played his part too, joining in the laughter and scoffing the buns.

But there was something.

As he painted the door frame that led down to the toilets Loaf's mind went back to when they were children, just seven or eight-years-old.

Loaf's mother had given them a few pence to go to the shop for chocolate.

After ten minutes of deciding what they wanted, he had gone to the counter to pay.

Outside he handed his cousin the Twix he had opted for, only to see Johnny produce two Curly Wurlys from the inside of his coat. Pilfered from under the nose of the shopkeeper.

Loaf looked at him, shocked. The two of them ran, eventually coming to a halt behind Heaney's Row.

Out of breath, they shouted at each other about the crime of the century that had just been committed.

Johnny's immediate reaction was to lie, to claim that he hadn't stolen them, that they had been in his pocket all along. But even then, the chocolate bars nearly as tall as the two scamps about to devour them, Loaf noticed his cousin's over-blinking.

Of course they were caught. Johnny's suspicious in-store behaviour had prompted a scan of the CCTV which told the till attendant all she needed to know.

When Johnny tried to wriggle his way out of trouble, his mother pointed out that she could always tell by his blinking that there was something going on.

It was an uncontrollable 'tell' that would give him away time and time again as he got older.

He was doing it again now, over-blinking any time his cousin asked how things were going or if he was okay.

There was something. And it was to do with Andy, a rat-faced character who would drop in now and again to speak to Johnny in private.

Loaf took an instant dislike to him, mainly because he had a tattoo on his right calf of a kneeling gunman with the words 'All Taigs are Targets', a reference to Northern Ireland's Catholic population.

When Andy was about, Loaf generally paid him little attention other than the odd nod of recognition.

That was until two days before opening when Andy overstepped the mark.

It happened as he and Johnny were getting ready to leave. Johnny had just ducked down to use the loo when his mate snorted a large glob of green phlegm from the bottom of his throat into his mouth and spat it on the floor, about two feet from where Abbey was brushing.

Loaf immediately confronted him about it.

'What are you playing at ya dirty animal? Clean that up.'

'That's your job mop monkey,' said Andy with a snarling laugh. 'Or what about your girlfriend there, maybe she'll clean it. I heard she likes being on her knees.'

Just as Loaf was about to make a run at him, Johnny came bounding up the stairs.

'What's going on here?'

'Your pal there spat on the floor and is refusing to clean it up.'

'Andy what are you playing at man,' asked Johnny in a pleading voice.

'Don't you fuckin' start. If I want to get up on top of that bar and piss all over this place then I'll do it.'

Johnny looked at a loss as to what to do. He decided the best course of action was to get Andy as far away from the pub as possible.

'Right Andy, are we ready to go? Shaun, clean that mess up and I'll chat to you in the morning. The good news is that the brewery has been and delivered kegs. Why don't you hook one up and have a couple of pints on the house. I'll see you all later.'

He and Andy left, slamming the front door behind them.

Abbey, Michael and Carl all turned to Loaf as if to ask 'what was that all about?'

Loaf looked at his watch. It was 4pm, an hour until clocking off time. He didn't want to talk about what had just happened, mainly because he hadn't a clue.

Who was this Andy bastard and what was his problem? He would get answers out of his cousin as soon as he saw him.

For now the mission was to defuse the tension in the room.

'As head barman I officially declare the working day over. Who's up for a beer?'

Four hands went up, including his own.

After hooking up a keg of Carling and turning on the gas, Loaf returned to pull the first pints in the newly resurrected Thirsty Sailor.

'Cheers guys,' he announced, clinking glasses with his workmates and taking a long hungry gulp of lager.

One pint became two which became three. The drinks kept flowing until Michael pointed out that it was almost 9pm.

A train of dirty pint glasses lined the bar counter.

'Holy shit, we'd better call it a night. I think we've all had enough anyway,' said Loaf.

Michael and Carl disagreed. Wednesday night was student night at Rocky's, the sports bar up at Onchan. They phoned a taxi and managed to convince Loaf to let them have one more pint while they waited.

Abbey was perched on a stool with a silly grin on her face. Leaning forward with her elbow on the bar counter and her chin resting on her fist she looked at him and giggled, 'I am sooooo drunk. I need to go home.'

'We need to go home you mean,' replied Loaf, trying to present himself as sober.

When the taxi came, the driver agreed to send another car along to take the two remaining stragglers to Westfield Terrace.

Loaf still had enough wit about him to make sure everything was turned off and that the place was properly locked up.

They only had to wait a few minutes for their cab, the two of them climbing into the back seat.

'Thank you for taking me home,' said Abbey, reaching for his hand.

'It's a little bit out of my way but as they say, a friend in need is a friend indeed,' he joked.

His heart was thumping as they neared Westfield Terrace. What to do? He knew where things might potentially go but she was so drunk. Imagine if she got up the next morning and claimed he had taken advantage of her? He could end up in a world of trouble.

The taxi pulled up and Loaf handed the driver a tenner, telling him to keep the change.

He got out and went around to open the door on Abbey's side.

'Thank you Shaun Donnelly. And rest assured, I'm not as drunk as I might appear. Now what about one more beer before we hit the hay. Separately of course, you in your bed, me in mine.'

He had bought in a box of Heineken in case the notion took him for a bottle some evening.

'Fair enough. But one beer and then you're going to your apartment, do you hear me?'

'Yes boss,' she laughed as she swayed up the steps.

Loaf looked in the direction of the hedge. There was no sign of Magnus who no doubt would have had questions had he seen the situation that was developing yards from his lookout post.

Upstairs Abbey threw herself down on the sofa and kicked off her shoes.

Loaf cracked open two bottles of beer and handed her one.

'So tell me your plans Mr Donnelly. Is this it, the Isle of Man for the rest of your days?'

'I don't know. I've only just got here and it's been non-stop work since I arrived. When I get a bit of time I'll have a look around and see what I think.'

'You know what you should do, you should take the train up to Port Erin. It's stunning and there's a diner up there that does the best fish and chips you will ever taste.'

'Port Erin? I'll put it on my list,' he replied, sitting himself down on a chair.

Night-time radio provided the soundtrack as they sipped Heineken and chatted.

It was 1am before they decided to turn in.

'Right Miss Abbey, it's your bedtime,' he said standing up. 'In fact it was your bedtime about three hours ago but here we are. My head is going to be banging in the morning.'

Getting up off the sofa, she moved over and kissed him on the lips.

'I'm not sure I can make it up the stairs. I might have to stay here tonight if that's okay with you,' she said softly.

HIS alarm went off at 7.30am.

He opened one eye and waited for the world to tell him how he felt.

Just okay was the initial diagnosis as he lay staring at the ceiling. Suddenly he was hit by a tidal waves of memories – Andy the bastard, the session in the pub and then beers in the flat with Abbey. And then kissing Abbey. And then Abbey in his bed…

He rubbed his face as a million thoughts peppered his heavy, cloudy brain. As he did so he caught the distinct smell of condom rubber on his hands.

It was surprising as he didn't have any. Abbey must have had one in her bag.

At least we had the sense to use it, he told himself.

He had to pee but his attempt to get out of bed without disturbing her proved unsuccessful.

'You weren't sneaking off without saying goodbye were you,' she asked in a husky morning voice.

'We're in my flat so I'm not sure where I would be sneaking to,' he answered, sitting on the edge of the bed in his boxer shorts.

'Urghhh, I was so wasted last night. Why didn't you kick me upstairs to my own bed?'

'Because you were so wasted and you wouldn't go.'

'That does sound like me in fairness,' Abbey admitted, turning around in the bed to look at him. 'Any chance of a cup of coffee? Then I'll go up and get a shower and we'll walk down to the bar together, how does that sound?'

'That sounds spot on. We're almost done anyway, only a few minor things left to iron out. But we should be good to go by tomorrow night.'

'Tomorrow is my last full day on the island, I fly to Heathrow on Saturday and then on to Toronto. I'm going to miss this place so much. I would love to stay and see how The Thirsty Sailor works out. I reckon it's going to be a big success.'

'I hope so. It's a pity you can't stay on for another while.'

'I can't. I have to get back and register for the new semester. The sooner this course is behind me the better. I don't even want to do law, it's my dad who is making me study it. I think he sees me taking over the firm one day.'

With her back to him she got up out of bed completely naked. On her right shoulder she had a tattoo of a butterfly.

She pulled on her pants and her t-shirt and ran her fingers through her hair.

'I don't hear a kettle boiling mister,' she smiled flirtatiously, brushing past him.

Chapter Seven

The plan was to open the doors at 5pm.

Michael and Carl had been sent to Strand Street to hand out fliers inviting the public to the all-new Thirsty Sailor and informing them there was live music and two-for-one on certain spirits.

Loaf used their absence to speak to his cousin about the confrontation with Andy.

'What's the story with you and him then? Why are you hanging about with an ignorant pig like that?'

'He's just someone I know, that's all.'

'Come on Johnny, we both know that's not true.'

'I don't want to talk about it Shaun alright, just leave it.'

'Fair enough. But I'm the head barman here and he's first on the list to be barred.'

'You can't bar him. Andy stays, do you hear me,' Johnny shouted.

The outburst caught Loaf by surprise. But he didn't flinch as his cousin frowned at him.

'What's got into you? In the short time I've been here you've gone from being like a child at Christmas to being like this, like you're carrying the world on your shoulders.'

'I'm sorry cuz, it's just that I'm under a bit of pressure with getting this place ready and all. You don't have to worry about Andy okay? I've had a word with him and told him to wind his neck in.'

'Johnny, you know you can tell me anything, don't you? Me and you, we're blood. Remember the Halloween we built the bonfire in the field behind your house? I climbed to the top to put up the flag with our names on it and ended up falling all the way down. You ran to your house screaming that I was dead. The look of relief on your mum's face when she saw me sitting up, alive and well apart from a dislocated shoulder.

'It never fully mended you know, I still get the odd twinge even now.'

'I'll never forget you coming down that bonfire. You were like a ragdoll, you must have bounced off every tyre and pallet,' Johnny recalled with a smile.

After a momentary pause, he added, 'I'll be fine. And Shaun, thank you.'

'For what?'

'For being sound. You've always been a good friend to me and if truth be told there have been plenty of days when I wished I was more like you – straight, honest, hardworking. But that's not who I am. Me and bother, I think we're just destined to see out our time together.'

'I don't know about that. You've an opportunity here to shake it off and put your past behind you. Your folks will be very proud when they see what you've achieved.'

The conversation was broken by Michael and Carl returning from advertising duties.

'How did you get on,' asked Johnny.

'Great. Loads of people told us they would call in for a drink later.'

'Excellent,' Johnny replied. Looking at his watch, he announced, 'Let's get this place open and packed because I have about a thousand people with their hands out looking to be paid.'

They were still a quarter of an hour from showtime and Loaf insisted that they do one final run-through. He checked the pumps to make sure the beer was flowing while Michael inspected the toilets. Carl was told to give the tables one last clean.

At 5pm The Thirsty Sailor opened to the waiting world.

Or not waiting, as the case turned out to be.

To their disappointment there wasn't a single person on the other side of the front door. Literally not a soul. They were all convinced that there would be a queue down the street waiting to see Douglas's newest hotspot.

'Give them half an hour. Once they get finished up at work they'll be along,' remarked Johnny, an anxious look on his face.

Loaf hoped that Abbey might call in.

After leaving his flat she had gone up to get showered and changed.

They had walked to work together, Abbey a little delicate and deliberately avoiding any talk of their night of passion. He had hoped they might grab lunch together and maybe discuss what had happened. But every time an opportunity presented itself she seemed to find another job to do. At 5pm she had almost run out the door, claiming she had some shopping to do. Shopping. She was leaving in less than 48 hours, what could she need?

Loaf told himself he was imagining it, that she wasn't swerving him. But she was and he had no idea why. It hurt.

He had only been in love once before. With Evelyn. And what a mess he had made of that.

Pull yourself together Shaun Joseph Donnelly, he scolded as he stood at the bar's hatch awaiting The Thirsty Sailor's first customer.

His emotional dissection of himself was interrupted by a middle-aged couple putting away the umbrellas they had been using to fend off the drizzle that had settled over Douglas.

'I'll have a pint of Guinness and Eileen you'll have a gin and tonic?'

'Oh yes please and ice with a slice of lemon.'

Looking around them they marvelled at how well the place looked.

'I remember this place when it was The Scottish,' remarked Eileen. 'A guy called Dominic had it. Became his own best customer in the end, drank himself out of it. That was years ago and as far as I know it has been empty since. Until now of course.'

Any fears that opening night might be a flop quickly dissipated as more and more people rolled in.

By 10 pm the band was in full swing and the bar was packed.

Loaf was just about to tell Johnny he was taking ten minutes to himself when he spotted Abbey and a group of her friends shuffling through the front door.

They managed to edge their way to the bar counter where she ordered a large vodka and Coke and a round of tequilas.

'No problem,' said Loaf, having to raise his voice to be heard over the din. 'I was thinking, would you mind if I go with you to the airport tomorrow?'

One of the friends overheard him.

Nudging Abbey and laughing, she asked annoyingly, 'Ooooh, what's going on here then?'

'Nothing Shauna, nothing's going on.' Turning her attention back to Loaf, she added, 'Why would you come to the airport with me?'

'I was just thinking, you know…after the other night.'

'The other night,' she blurted out through laughter. Looking at him like someone might look at a wounded puppy, she added, 'That's so cute. But Shaun, it was just sex, a bit of fun.'

His heart hit the floor with a thud.

Somehow he managed to keep his composure. With an admirable façade of nonchalance, he replied cooly, 'Yeah I know that. I just thought you might need someone to help you with your luggage.'

'It's fine, Simon is driving me. But thank you for the offer, it's very sweet.'

Simon? He had no idea who Simon was but the way she said his name, it told him he was a boyfriend of sorts.

She turned away as if she had already forgotten him.

'Right girls, are we getting this party started or what,' she shouted, handing out tequilas.

Abbey and her friends stayed for about an hour before moving on. He watched as she left without giving him as much as a wave.

He was still staring at the front door when a voice called his name.

'Hi, give me a pint of Stella please.'

It was Andy the bastard. Loaf pulled the beer pump without saying a word, half hoping that Andy would give him a reason to smack him. The mood he was in, there was a good chance he would end up on a murder charge.

'I'm sorry about the last day,' said Andy. 'I was out of order and it won't happen again.'

'No problem,' muttered Loaf, only half listening.

'You'll be seeing me around here quite a lot so it's only right that we go forward on good terms.'

'Yeah. That's £2.80 please,' he responded, still only half tuned in.

The rest of the evening flew by. It was 12.30am when they pulled the door and gave everyone half an hour to drink up.

It was 1.25am by the time they got the last person out. It was going to take at least another hour and a half to get the place cleaned, stocked and ready for opening again. Bar work was no country for old men, thought Loaf as he looked at the mess that stretched out before him.

Before the clear up started they all sat down for ten minutes to weigh up the night's events.

Johnny, delighted at the empty shelves and bulging till drawer, was already pouring staff pints.

'At one stage I thought I was going to have to close the doors, there was that many in here,' he crowed.

Eventually the mop buckets fell silent and the last bottle was placed in the fridge.

'Well done guys. We should all be very proud,' said Johnny, glugging down the last of his beer.

'Michael and Carl, Loaf and I will talk about a rota tomorrow morning. I know you two are at college so let us know when you are available okay? And Loaf, we'll have to try and get another couple of people on the payroll. If you see any potential candidates, take their details and we'll do our best to give them a few shifts.'

They all agreed that opening night had been a success.

Pulling on their jackets, Johnny offered to leave everyone home in the van.

Michael and Carl accepted while Loaf opted to walk because 'the fresh air will do me good'.

The real reason was that he was hoping to bump into a drunk Abbey making her way home.

Twenty five minutes later he reached number 12 Westfield Terrace. There was a red Audi parked outside with the number plate 'Sim4n'.

He glanced at his watch. It was 3.25am.

As he looked up he saw a faint light in her apartment window go out.

⸺◈⟨▷⟩◈⸺

Chapter Eight

The Thirsty Sailor quickly settled into a busy little groove. It had a steady stream of regulars through the week and plenty of young night-time revellers at the weekend.

Among the faces that frequented it was Lilly Armstrong, a hairy-chinned old lady who needed two walking sticks to keep her upright.

Lilly's son would bring her into town on a Tuesday and Thursday where she would collect her pension and do her shopping before getting absolutely blitzed in the bar.

Cinzano and peppermint was her tipple, two drinks Loaf had never once encountered back home.

Lilly would pick a few horses before snagging someone to walk up to the bookies for her.

Her afternoon would then be spent watching the racing through a Cinzano and peppermint haze.

Among Lilly's less appealing habits were her farts which she found hilarious and her singing which was terrible. There was never any warning given of either. One minute she would be sitting silently and the next she would be blasting out Goldfinger by Shirley Bassey.

At 7pm on the button Ian, her son, would come and pick her up, never complaining, just making sure she was okay.

Declan 'Knickers' McKenzie was another one who had found a new home in The Thirsty Sailor.

A friendly if somewhat disturbed character, Knickers was so-called because he'd once been caught stealing underwear off next door's washing line. Apparently the whole episode had been documented in The Manx Chronicle which had reported how he had been fined £75 and ordered not to go near the convent again.

Gary 'Two Tellies' Morrison was usually about as well.

His nickname flowed from the fact that he walked with his two arms away from his body, as if he had a telly under each arm. Gary fancied himself as a hard man but at little over five feet in height it was impossible to take him seriously.

The appealing thing about Two Tellies was the counterfeit clothes he was always trying to sell. No one knew where he sourced the stuff but he could usually be found with a box full of fake hoodies, t-shirts or sunglasses. And they were generally of decent enough quality.

'Look at these, brand new Hughie Vuitton handbags. You'd pay £1,500 for one of these, I'm letting them go for £25. Treat the missus, go on.'

Bert Russell and his wife Angie were in most evenings.

Bert was on his third liver, the other two having been burnt out through drinking cheap cider. Doctors had warned him this was his last because livers didn't grow on trees. He had reluctantly heeded their advice. Bert hadn't consumed an alcoholic beverage of any description in eight years. His drink of choice now was apple juice which he tended to stare at glumly, probably wishing that he was still on lucky liver number two.

In an admirable display of non-solidarity with her melancholy mister, Angie Russell drank vodka and water as if vital organs did indeed blossom in some magical orchard somewhere.

Despite their issues, of which there appeared to be quite a few, Angie and Bert were good people and universally liked.

Less welcome among The Thirsty Sailor's regular patrons was a darker element that congregated from time to time, usually with Andy at its centre. Loaf hated to see them coming. They were loud, bad-mannered and disrespectful. He also believed they were selling drugs but as of yet he had no evidence to back up his suspicions.

All in all, The Sailor wasn't a bad place to work. It was bright and airy, it was about 30 seconds from the beach and most importantly, it seemed to be turning a profit.

For reasons that he was still keeping to himself though, Johnny was fretting.

'Hopefully we'll have a good TT,' he said more than once as the biggest weekend on the island's festival calendar neared.

ABBEY had left without saying goodbye.

He had heard voices and the trundle of suitcases across the hall followed by a car engine starting up. He hadn't bothered getting up to look. It was just a shag, a bit of fun, isn't that what she had told him?

He had sulked silently for a couple of days, at his lowest point he had even considered throwing in the towel and returning to Ballyrush.

But summer was looming and the weather was improving with each passing day. Also, the prospect of working through the world famous Isle of Man TT road racing competition was too much to pass up.

Even his was mum was buzzing about it.

'Joey Dunlop, The King of the Mountain they called him,' she said over the phone. 'I remember meeting him the time he came to Ballyrush Leisure Centre. He was such a lovely man, God rest him. They show the TT on the telly over here you know. I'll be keeping an eye out for you.'

'I'll be working literally every day mum, I don't think I'll have time to get in front of the cameras.'

'Just you look after yourself son and steer clear of them bikes, they're dangerous. That cousin of yours, he's the kind of empty head who would have one.'

'A STRIP club, what do you think?'

'Johnny, you can't be serious.'

'Look, there's an advert here,' he said, jabbing his finger at one of the English tabloids. 'They want to bring some of their page three models over for TT week. I was thinking of offering them this place.'

'But we've only been opened a wet weekend. Let's get ourselves established first and maybe we can look at it for next year.'

'Loaf, where is your sense of adventure? It'll be great craic.'

Johnny Donnelly had been accused of many things in his life. Being boring or predictable were two charges he would never have to answer.

According to the advertisement the promoters were looking for a venue for seven nights. And they were willing to pay £5,000 to hire it.

All his years working in The Barking Dog and the closest Loaf had come to a strip joint was the night Samantha Rice's strapless dress had malfunctioned. It was a revealing misfortune that was still talked about to this day.

Johnny was dancing with excitement now, his face like that of a child who had just been told they were going to Disneyland for their birthday.

'Tell me we are going to make this happen,' he begged.

Loaf thought about it for another second before nodding his head to indicate he had been badgered into submission.

Then he blessed himself and hoped his mother would never find out.

THE build-up began on May 26 with qualifying week.

Extra boats were put on to ship competitors, fans, their motorcycles and their leather jackets on to the island.

At Ronaldsway Airport there were long queues as visitors flew in to enjoy the sporting spectacle.

The noise of revving bikes filled the air while every pub on the island was stocked to the teeth, staff steeling themselves for the onslaught of eager punters.

Only one though was preparing to welcome an ensemble of strippers.

Michael, Carl and new recruits Kelly and Izzy were understandably excited. Given that none of them were over 21, Loaf had taken the liberty of contacting their parents to let them know what has happening. The last thing he needed was a tearful mum or furious dad landing down claiming that their child's innocence had been snatched from them without their consent.

It was also made very clear that no one was under any obligation to work. If a staff member felt uncomfortable, arrangements could be made to have their shifts covered.

'No chance,' said a giggling Kelly. 'I want to see what all the fuss is about.'

As head barman it was Loaf's job to make sure everything went smoothly. So just before kick-off he puffed out his chest, put on his serious face and gathered his team together.

'Right boys and girls, it is going to be really busy tonight. I need you all to stay focussed on the customers. The ladies will do their thing, your job is to serve drink and put money in the till.'

At 9pm three beefy bouncers took up position at the door. The lights were dimmed as six women, all naked apart from g-strings and bras, paraded in.

On the signal of one of the organisers, Loaf pressed a button that sent smooth R&B dance music to the speakers.

The system was straight forward – customers could sit and watch for free or if they wanted a lap dance they stuck a £20 note in the air and waited their turn.

Each performer was accompanied by a security guard who made sure there was no touching. The minders also carried with them a box of Kleenex tissues, should anyone get a little too excited.

Only Izzy needed an explanation as to why.

'You are joking me,' the young bartender remarked with an appalled look on her face. 'That might be the grossest thing I've ever heard in my life.'

The demand for drinks was huge, every staff member struggling to keep up with the endless stream of orders.

Michael almost had to be worked with when one of the women, a 6'2" model named Pandora, put her leg up on the bar, narrowly missing him with her high heel. It wasn't so much the heel that caused him to feel lightheaded, but the fact that Pandora was as naked as the day she was born.

Loaf wept tears of laughter as his young colleague struggled to keep his composure.

As he prepared a Horny Momma cocktail Loaf looked around him. Two months ago The Thirsty Sailor was a boarded up corpse of a building. Tonight it was a throbbing hotbed of sex, booze and money.

'You creep, put that away,' shouted one of the girls at a grinning punter who had unzipped his jeans to reveal his manhood.

Amid much cheering and clapping from his pals, security stepped in to walk him to the door.

'This is crazy,' Loaf shouted to Johnny who was doubled over with glee, having watched the vulgar episode through a gap in the fingers he had thrown over his eyes.

But as the night pressed on, the novelty began to wear off. The queue for liquor was unconquerable, the music increasingly unbearable and the customers more and more lairy.

By the end, everyone was running on empty.

It was after 2am before the last paying guest left, stumbling their way out on to Douglas prom.

The strippers stayed for a drink, chatting away about the night's events.

Loaf looked around him. The scene was pure art. His staff looked like they had been in the trenches. Scattered among them were six stunning models who had spent the last four hours gyrating and pushing their selling points into the faces of salivating clients.

Kelly was in full conversation with them all, later revealing that one of the girls, Josie, was using the money to put herself through school.

'She's really lovely. She's studying nursing at Birmingham College. She even gave me her phone number.'

Carl, who at the start of the night was like a greyhound in heat, now looked like he needed put to sleep.

'We've run out everything,' he groaned. 'There's no Bacardi left, there's no change left, there's no toilet roll left. And this is only night one.'

To their relief Loaf revealed that a cleaner would be coming in first thing in the morning. And plans were in place for a visit to the cash and carry.

The week went by without further major incident. Another couple of customers had to be ejected for getting too hands-on. But apart from that there was nothing to report other than big laughs and big earnings.

They all breathed deeply when the door shut on the final night.

'You'll not forget that week in a hurry,' Loaf remarked to Michael, giving his exhausted colleague a friendly, well-earned pat on the back.

Chapter Nine

The agreement was that after TT fortnight the bar would stay closed for two days to allow for a much needed recharge of the batteries.

Loaf rang his cousin and told him they were going to Port Erin.

'So what if you've never been to it? Neither have I. It'll be a surprise for both of us. Come and get me in an hour. You drive, I'll buy lunch.'

As they motored through the Manx countryside Loaf asked, 'Have you been in the counting house yet, was TT fortnight the financial success you hoped it would be?'

'It was good. It could have been better but sure things could always be better.'

Loaf's face turned red with fury.

'Pull over.'

'What are you on about?'

'Pull this van over Johnny or I'll take that steering wheel and put us both off the road.'

Johnny stopped abruptly in a layby, at a loss as to why his cousin was upset.

They both got out.

'You are going to tell me now what is going on or I swear to God I'll kick you from here to Ballyrush.'

'Nothing's going on.'

'Yes it is Johnny, I can tell. Every time I ask you a question you start blinking like a man possessed. You left Ireland with hardly a penny in your pocket and you've come over and mysteriously managed to start your own business. This last two weeks we've worked our balls to the bone and you still have the cheek to tell me it could have been better? You're a fucking prick, that's what you are.'

Johnny stared sheepishly at the ground, pushing the gravel around with his foot. Then he sat down on the edge of the kerb and looked out towards the sea.

Not a word was spoken for a full two minutes.

It was Johnny who eventually broke the silence.

'Why does trouble follow me Shaun? Why me? It never bothers you, oh no it leaves you well alone. Me? I'm tortured with the fucker.'

Sitting down beside him, Loaf picked up a stone and threw it into the field across the road.

'You may tell me all about it then.'

Over the next 30 minutes Johnny took him back, explaining about the drugs bust in the car wash years earlier and the various other incidents that had landed him in court.

'I was a fool. I let people talk me into things I shouldn't have been anywhere near. But you know the worst of it? Seeing what my stupidity did to my mother. It worried her half to death. I don't know how many nights I heard her sobbing in her bed because of me.

'My father, he just got angry. We would shout at each other, him telling me how he had worked hard and honest his whole life. I would argue back that I wasn't him, that I was my own man. I was such an idiot.

'Then one day I arrived home and the oul fella said he needed a serious chat.'

'What did he want,' asked Loaf, engrossed in the story he was being told.

'He wanted to give me £75,000. He told me they had sold the cottage in Donegal and that if I wanted, he could give me my inheritance early. But on the condition that I get out of Ballyrush.

'That was hard to hear. My own father basically telling me that he wanted me out of his sight. You know how much they loved that cottage in Glencolmcille. How many summers did you and I spend in it when we were little? And they decided to sell it because of me.'

'You took the money though.'

'I had no choice. My parents wanted me to go and If I had stayed I would have ended up in prison. If that had happened I genuinely believe it would have killed my mother. I took the cash, had a look around and found this place, the Isle of Man, far enough away but not so far either.'

It was quite the tale and listening to it, Loaf started to feel sorry for his cousin. He was right, he was an idiot. But more to be pitied than feared.

Johnny explained how when he first arrived on the island he had booked himself into a guesthouse, paying £25 per night for bed and breakfast. After finding a flat to rent he began scouting around for work and opportunities.

'You know me, always looking to make a pound. I saw the bar and the faded 'for lease' sign on it. I never for a second thought that £75,000 would get me in the door but I spoke to the estate agent anyway. She contacted the owner, some guy in Berlin who was left the place in his uncle's will. He wanted rid of it and couldn't sign the lease agreement quick enough.

'I was on top of the world until I realised that, as usual, I was somewhere I had no errand being – with my own pub and no real clue what to do with it. That's when I called you.'

'Your number one cousin.'

'My number one cousin. You know Shaun all I wanted to do when I came here was to fix things, to build something that would make my parents proud of me again. I even had visions of buying them a new cottage in Donegal one day.'

Out of the side of his eye Loaf could see his cousin was getting emotional. He tried to reassure him.

'And you're doing well,' he said in a soothing voice. 'The Thirsty Sailor is up and running and from what I can see, it's turning a pound.'

'Thank God because I've steeped everything I have in it. But wait until you hear this. You remember the day you arrived, we had dinner and I left you home? That evening I went back to the bar, for no particular reason other than I was excited because it was me and you and our wee project.

'I was sitting there with a big dopey grin on my face when a knock came to the door. I opened it and there was Andy. I had no idea who he was or what he wanted but he had a Northern Ireland accent and he seemed friendly enough. I invited him in, showed him the place, made him a cup of coffee. He asked me if I'd heard of his boss, a guy called Charlie Harrison.'

Charlie Harrison. The name had come up once or twice in the bar but always accompanied by nervous glances in case unwanted ears heard what was being said.

'Andy said Harrison was keen to meet with me. He said he was a businessman who liked to shake the hand of anyone opening a premises in Douglas. I thought he must be one of these Chamber of Commerce sorts so I said of course, I'd love to have a chat.

'That was fine, we arranged to meet in The Bingham Hotel.

'A few nights later I went along. It was about 7pm when Andy came in with this guy walking slightly behind him. He was wearing grey trousers, a white shirt and a grey suit jacket, smart casual you might call it. He had a bad limp whatever was wrong with him and he was using a cane for support. But you know who he looked a bit like?'

'Who?'

'Granda.'

'Granda? Our granda?'

'Aye, Granda Donnelly. He was tall and thin and he had the same white hair and everything. Honestly, that's who he reminded me of.'

'Granda Donnelly was some man wasn't he,' said Loaf. 'What about that magic trick he used to do, the one where he would turn the fiver into a tenner. I never did work out how he did it.'

'Me neither. Remember after granny left him he took up with that one Marjorie from out by Ballinaleck? What a sight she was, you couldn't have drawn worse. But he thought she was a peach. As you say he was some man, God rest him.'

Johnny explained how it took Charlie Harrison a minute to get down into the chair on account of his mobility issues.

'He didn't give much away about himself at all. He said he was Manx born and bred and that he owns a casino. But that was it. He was more about asking questions - where I was from, what brought me to the Isle of Man, what I hoped to achieve and so on. At this stage I was still under the impression it was a friendly meet and greet. And to be honest he seemed okay at first.'

'At first? That sounds ominous.'

Sitting in the large foyer of The Bingham, Charlie Harrison took a sip from the glass of sparkling water Andy had gone to the bar to get him.

He had a gold tooth where one of his front incisors used to be. Pinned to his lapel was a Pioneer Pin, an indication that he abstained from alcohol.

Johnny wondered what age he was. Late 60s, early 70s maybe.

After about ten minutes of questions, Harrison's tone began to change, becoming more serious.

Leaning forward in his chair, he placed the glass on the table and lowered his voice.

'Okay son, enough small talk. This is how it works. I run this town. Understand?'

The question caught Johnny off-guard.

'Not really, no,' he replied honestly.

'The bookies, the barbers, the takeaways, the launderettes, the pubs, even Fran's Flower Shop, they are all open because of me, because I allow them to stay open. I'm generous like that. But my generosity comes at a price.'

Johnny looked at him with a lost expression. Harrison stared coldly back at him. There was a hardness in his eyes that said he would shoot a man dead and go for a steak afterwards.

He wasn't like Granda Donnelly at all, thought Johnny, his mind racing as to where all this was going.

'Here is how it works. A business of the size of your bar, it's turning over what, £5,000 a week? I charge ten per-cent.'

'Ten per-cent for what?'

Harrison looked at Andy and laughed.

'Where did you get this one Andrew? You wouldn't just be the brightest light in the street would you son? Ten per-cent for protection.'

'Okay. But protection from what?'

'Jesus wept, do I have to spell it out? From what will happen if I don't get my ten per-cent. Andrew, details please.'

'Ten per-cent of £5,000 is £500 which I will collect from you, in cash, every Sunday night. This is non-negotiable. Miss a payment at your peril. Understand?'

Johnny wanted out of there. He had thought the meeting was to welcome him to the Douglas business community. How wrong he had been.

'Okay Mr Harrison, I'll think about it,' he said, looking at his watch as if he had somewhere else to be.

As he got up to go Andy grabbed him by the wrist.

'Sit down.'

'You'll think about it, is that what you just said,' growled Harrison. 'What part of non-negotiable did you not understand? You'll have my money for me every Sunday night or else.'

'And there's one other thing.'

The crime boss went on to explain that Andy, or Andrew as he liked to refer to him, would be selling 'certain substances' in The Thirsty Sailor.

'You don't have to worry about the cops, I have them covered. Just you and your staff look the other way and everything will be fine.'

'Look Mr Harrison I would rather not…'

Ignoring the incoming plea to be left in peace, Harrison reached for his cane and started to get up.

'I think that's everything Andrew. Welcome to the Isle of Man Mr Donnelly, I'll be in touch.'

LOAF stared at his cousin with a look of incredulity as he relayed the details of the meeting.

'You have to pay protection money to this header? That's mental.'

'And his men are selling gear in the bar.'

As Loaf had suspected.

'Fuck me,' he said with a shake of his head.

'I know, that's why I'm so stressed Shaun. That's why I look like shit.'

Loaf tried to come up with something that might help the situation. But instead of comforting words he burst out laughing.

'What are you laughing about,' asked Johnny, the tears glistening on his cheeks. 'It's not funny.'

'I'm laughing because it's mad, completely mad. You left home with the sole intention of going straight, to make your folks proud. And here you are with some hoodlum's shiny winklepicker on your throat. If it wasn't for bad luck you would have no luck at all JD.'

'Tell me about it,' replied a disconsolate Johnny.

'Right, get in the van,' ordered Loaf, punching his cousin on the arm.

'Where are we going?'

'I hear there's a diner in Port Erin that does the best fish and chips in the Isle of Man. I don't know about you but I'm starving.'

AT first blush Port Erin was just another village.

The main street was standard fare – an estate agent, a pub or two, a couple of hairdressers, a charity shop and a convenience store. There was a railway station, which was a novelty for two lads from a town that hadn't heard a train's whistle in over 40 years.

As they climbed down from the van Johnny's phone started to ring.

Looking at his mobile, he said it was a call he had to take and that it was probably going to be a while.

'Go for a walk and meet me back here in 15 minutes.'

Loaf rolled his eyes and shook his head. He had no other option than to go and explore.

Around the corner and just a few yards further on it became apparent that Port Erin was not just another village.

Stretching out before him was a stunning blue and green panorama where rugged hills rolled down to shining sea.

In school his favourite story had always been the one about Tír na nÓg, the mythical land where no one grew old.

One time the teacher had instructed his class to draw what they imagined Tír na nÓg might look like.

A ten-year-old Loaf had drawn this, right down to the castle up there on the peak.

After making his way down to the beach he stopped to take off his socks and shoes and then laughed as the sand tickled his toes.

Sitting himself down he watched a canoeist padel gracefully across the bay, completely at ease on her lone nautical adventure.

Anchored sailboats bobbed gently, their names visible and then invisible as the tides softly toyed with them – The Kingfisher, The Ark, The Sugrue.

A little way along and three elderly women were enjoying tea and buns around a portable table they had brought with them.

He didn't want to leave. Every part of him wanted to remain in his Tír na nÓg, far away from the noisy, ceaseless jackhammer of civilisation.

But he had to go back.

'If I ever come into money this is where I'm retiring to,' Loaf vowed to himself, even picking out the house on the hill that he would buy should his numbers one day come up.

OVER lunch they talked briefly about Charlie Harrison but Loaf could see his cousin had had enough of the subject.

'How have you been getting on since you landed, are you missing Ballyrush at all,' asked Johnny, shovelling a forkful of mushy peas into his mouth.

'Not really. I miss my mum but I speak to her a couple of times a week on the phone and she's fine.'

'Have you any women on the go that I should know about?'

'Nah. There was one but she's gone now.'

'Come on, spill.'

'It was Abbey, you know the Canadian one who helped us in the bar at the start.'

'No way. Abbey Vincent? Man I would eaten these chips out of her knickers. How did you pull her?'

Ignoring the crudeness of his cousin's remark, Loaf explained how she had been living in the flat upstairs from his own.

'We got drunk one night and she ended up staying in my place.'

'You jammy bastard. She was going with that spanner Simon Craig who owns the antique shop over in Jurby too. And how did you leave it with her?'

'I didn't really. After she stayed over we never spoke again. Between me and you I was a bit devastated because I really liked her. But it's all history now.'

'You know what you should do,' suggested Johnny, pointing his fork in his cousin's direction to emphasise his point. 'You should look her up on Facebook.'

'Facebook? What's that?'

'It's this new thing on the internet. You set up an account and you can connect with people all over the world.'

'Sounds expensive.'

'Expensive? It's free. Some students in America invented it and now everybody's at it. Get yourself down to Douglas library one of these days, get on a computer and set up a Facebook account. I'll bet you any money you'll find Abbey on there.'

Loaf was suddenly in better form.

'I'll have to get on this Facebook. Look, see this Charlie Harrison character, what if you just tell him to fuck off? Tell him you'll go to the police if he doesn't leave you alone.'

'He's a drug baron Loaf, not some neighbour whose dog keeps shitting on my lawn. I'd be fish food in two minutes if I tried to threaten him with the cops.'

'I suppose so. Look, we'll keep putting one foot in front of the other for now and see where it takes us.'

'It's all we can do,' replied Johnny.

Running his last chip around his plate and into a splodge of tomato ketchup, he added, 'See that blinking, that has been the bane of my life you know.'

Chapter Ten

'It's my birthday today,' called Magnus as Loaf came down the front steps.

'Is it? Happy birthday Magnus.'

'I'm 85-years-old. They're having a little party for me later. Will you be attending?'

Something akin to a friendship had developed between them, a daily exchange of words, usually about the weather.

Loaf hadn't much else to do on what was shaping up to be a lazy Tuesday.

'Yeah, why not? What time?'

'About 2pm. It'll just be the staff, a few of the other inmates, a cake and some of those little cocktail sausages. Unless you can find a couple of good looking young ladies who want to make an old man very happy.'

'I'm good but I'm not a miracle worker Magnus. I'll call in for a cuppa, how does that sound?'

'That sounds most excellent Shaun, thank you.'

With a wave Loaf headed off in the direction of town. His 'to do' list for the day had just doubled from the single entry of 'visit local library and see what this Facebook is all about'.

It was a few weeks since he'd spoken at any great length to Johnny. On the way back from Port Erin his cousin had revealed that after all the bills had been paid, TT fortnight had netted The Thirsty Sailor around £28,000.

The summer months should look after itself. What lay beyond that was anyone's guess.

'The bastard,' was how Johnny had angrily described Harrison as they drove. 'Imagine putting shit like this on us, fellas working their nuts off to make an honest living. And that's not even the biggest worry, the biggest worry is that the cops will get wind of the fact that Andy and his scummy pals are selling drugs. They'll shut us down for sure.'

DOUGLAS library was busy with what appeared to be a mother and baby group.

A brightly-dressed woman with pigtails was reading a story about a friendly dog to toddlers who were being encouraged to join her in performing the actions and sounds.

'And Toby jumped with a woof, woof, woof…' she told them, mimicking the leaping pooch, much to the delight of her wide-eyed audience.

The librarian, Shanice according to her name tag, looked over her glasses as Loaf approached the counter.

'Can I help you,' she asked.

'I was hoping to use a computer if that's okay,' he stuttered nervously.

'Are you a member of the library?'

'No. I've only moved here and haven't got around to joining yet.'

'I see. Here is a membership form, fill it in and leave it back when you're done. You won't be able to take out any books until you've joined but you can avail of our technology suite. It is located on the first floor, just up those stairs over there.'

The splendidly named 'technology suite' was a bland square room which housed a dozen or so computers, only one of which was free.

He sat himself down in the empty seat which creaked noisily under his weight, drawing an annoyed sideward glance from the scholarly looking man next to him.

As he settled himself Loaf looked across to see what his neighbour was reading. It was a website about the French Renaissance. Compared to it, his mission to locate a woman he barely knew in a country a million miles away seemed a bit childish and daft.

I've come this far I might as well have a look, he told himself as the urge quickened in him to get up and leave.

He clicked on the familiar 'internet' icon which brought up the Google search engine.

So far, so good, he thought to himself. He typed in Facebook, pressed 'Return' and waited as the machine processed his instruction.

After clicking on the link for the site he found himself for the second time in ten minutes being asked to fill in a form, this one digital rather than paper.

One question led to another and then another until he thought he was never going to get to his desired destination.

What is your name?

Where do you live?

What is your date of birth?

What is your occupation?

Tell us your favourite movie genre?

What music do you like?

How would you describe your relationship status: Single. Married. Divorced. Engaged. In a relationship. It's complicated.

The cops wouldn't ask you as many bloody questions, he grumbled impatiently while hovering over the box beside 'single'.

He watched as the little rainbow-coloured disc spun, indicating that the machine was crunching the data it had just been fed.

Finally a message flashed up – 'Welcome to Facebook'.

'Yes,' he exclaimed quietly but still too loudly for the studious gentleman next door who threw him another dirty look.

The site then suggested he add a photograph of himself.

'A photo? What the hell,' he muttered, relieved to see a 'Maybe Later' option.

'Let's starting adding friends,' was Facebook's next great idea.

Who do I know would be on this, he wondered.

After a short trawl through his brain, it came to him.

Into the search bar he typed the name 'Naomi Donnelly'.

It threw him up a long list of Naomi Donnellys. But he didn't have to scroll far to find the one he was looking for.

The photo was of his sister and one of her friends at a music festival, the both of them holding strawberry daiquiri cocktails and pulling silly faces for the camera.

He clicked 'Add Friend'. Almost instantly an alert appeared in the top right corner of the screen. He opened it to read 'You and Naomi Donnelly are now connected. Why not send each other a message'.

Before he had time to digest the information a chat box popped up.

'Big bro, you're on Facebook! I don't believe it!!xx'

He smiled and folded his arms. Modern technology really was something.

'Isn't that brilliant,' he observed with a chuckle.

'Yes I am,' typed Loaf back to his sister.

'Woohoo! How very exciting!! You need to upload a photo, I haven't seen your grumpy old face in ages'.

'I will,' he wrote, with no clue as to how he would get the spare passport photograph in his wallet into the computer.

'Cool. We'll be in touch loads now that we're Facebook buddies. Take care big bro. Super excited!!!!xx'

Chuffed that Naomi was so happy to hear from him, he moved on to the reason he was there in the first place.

Into the search bar this time he typed the name 'Abbey Vincent'.

Up popped a screen full of Abbey Vincents, with the navigation bar down the side telling him there was more. Lots more.

His heart sank at the seemingly endless list of profiles. It would take ages to wade through them all.

But then an idea occurred to him.

These were Abbey Vincents from all corners of the world. His Abbey Vincent was from Canada. And not just from Canada but from Saint John.

Re-energised, he quickly typed in 'Abbey Vincent Saint John Canada'.

Rather than hundreds of pages, this time Facebook showed just nine.

Jackpot, he thought to himself as he began scouring the list in front of him.

Only one had a photograph of an actual person. The others had flowers and pets as their profile pictures, some had nothing at all.

The woman who had posted a photo of herself was not his Abbey Vincent, the one with a butterfly tattoo on her shoulder.

There was only one way to go about it.

'Are you the Abbey Vincent who worked in a bar in the Isle of Man,' he wrote in a message to the first profile before copying, pasting and sending it to everyone.

He waited, expecting an instant response in the same way Naomi had answered him.

But when a minute passed, then two minutes and then five minutes, he started to get frustrated.

'Why is no one getting back to me? All I'm looking for is a yes or a no,' he mumbled grouchily.

After 30 minutes of disappointment, he decided to throw in the towel.

Looking at his watch he realised it was 1pm. Magnus's party was in an hour.

'Shit, I need to go and buy a card,' he declared, quickly logging out.

Grabbing his jacket and for no other reason than to piss him off again, he patted the man next to him on the shoulder and loudly wished him a good day.

THE care home was an assault on the senses.

The foyer was uncomfortably warm and smelt strongly of antiseptic and dinner. There was a reception desk, a row of wheelchairs and some plastic plants in need of dusting. The walls were painted beige, decorated with a cheap copy of Van Gogh's Starry Night and a large ornately framed photograph of some dignitaries cutting the ribbon on the home when it first opened.

As Loaf stood waiting to speak to a staff member, he heard a slow but steady metallic clacking sound coming up the corridor.

Its source was an elderly woman on a walking frame. She was wearing a flowery blouse, pink cardigan, brown trousers and brown bedroom slippers. Around her neck was a pair of glasses which she reached for on seeing him.

'Oh hello Raymond,' she said in a soft smiling voice. 'Have you seen my mum today?'

Loaf looked at her, lost for words. She was 90-years-old if she was a day.

Finding his voice, he replied as kindly as he could, 'I'm sorry, I haven't seen her.'

'Maybe she's gone to get something for our tea. I hope it's sausages, daddy and I love sausages. He works down at the docks you know.'

Loaf nodded gently but his speech was hampered by the lump in his throat. A tear of sadness was welling in his eye when a nurse came bustling up the corridor.

'Mrs Hampton, what are you doing out here on your own? You're supposed to be down in the common room.'

'I'm chatting to Raymond. I haven't seen him in such a long time.'

The nurse looked at Loaf with a roll of her eyes that he felt was slightly uncalled for. Then again, she probably had to deal with this sort of thing all day, every day.

'Okay Mrs Hampton, let's get you back to the rest of the group,' she suggested, guiding her patient gently down the corridor.

'Give me a minute and I'll be with you,' the nurse called over her shoulder.

'Okay. And bye Mrs Hampton, it was lovely to meet you,' he answered, meaning every word.

The encounter, brief as it was, hit him hard.

She was Mrs Hampton. But what was her first name? Maybe she was Sheila. Or Anne. Or June, named after the month of her birth perhaps. She had obviously lived a long life. She had seen the Second World War, maybe even World War One. There was a time when she had held her mum's hand on the way to her first day at school. During the holidays she had probably enjoyed going to the seaside with her parents and her siblings. She had had a first kiss, she had found a job, she had met the man who would later become her husband. There would have been a wedding day full of celebration and laughter. They had probably bought a house together and had children. It was likely there was a car in the driveway, maybe even a pet dog. How many evenings had Mrs Hampton admired the roses in her garden and smiled contentedly with a glass of wine in her hand as the sun went down?

Now she was here, in this place with its dusty fake plants and clammy, choking atmosphere that made you want to claw at your skin. She was here, roaming the corridors, calling strangers Raymond and asking about a mother who had likely been dead for 20 or 30 years. She was here, lost, her mind and memory gone, never to return.

Was this it? Was this what life had in store for him?

He felt like he was having a panic attack, his heart pounding in his chest like there was someone in there trying to escape.

Just as he was about to make a bolt for the door, he heard a friend's voice.

'Shaun, what are you doing standing out here? Come in before all the cake is gone.'

Chapter Eleven

Magnus was wearing a short sleeved shirt and a bowtie.

'Are you okay Shaun, you look very pale,' he asked.

Catching his breath, Loaf laughed a low grateful laugh.

'I'm fine Magnus, thank you. I don't know what came over me there. Nothing a cup of tea won't cure.'

Magnus signalled to follow him. As they walked down the corridor he called back, 'You said you were working in a bar? That's interesting.'

They turned left into a large communal area that was crackling with noise.

'Here we are,' said Magnus.

There were about 30 people seated on both sides of a trestle table which was lined with nibbles – mini sausage rolls, cocktail sausages, bitesize pizzas and a variety of biscuits and buns. Two staff members were busily filling plastic cups with blackcurrant juice and placing them in front of each party guest.

Coming through a speaker in the corner was John Denver singing Country Roads.

Loaf scanned the rest of the room. There were armchairs around its perimeter. In one of them was an elderly gentleman who was asleep. Two seats up from him a carer was spoon feeding a resident what looked like mashed potato and gravy.

Everyone else seemed to be having a good time. There was lots of laughing, swaying and singing on what otherwise would have been a very standard, mundane day. At the far end of the long table was a happy looking Mrs Hampton, Loaf noticed as Magnus returned with two mugs of tea.

'We'll sit over here, away from the crazy gang,' he said, handing over one of the cups before going to get a paper plate of cake and custard cream biscuits.

'All this, just for you,' said Loaf as they took their seats.

'It's usually somebody's birthday around here so this is fairly standard procedure,' replied Magnus. 'But it's nice because a lot of the residents don't have anyone. If it wasn't for the staff there would be no one to remind them that they're a year older.'

'And what about you Magnus, have you anyone?'

'Not anymore, not since my Josie passed. Twenty one years she's gone now and I miss her every single day.'

Loaf took a bite out of a custard cream and washed it down with a drink of his tea. The obvious question would have been 'what happened her'. But he sensed Magnus wanted to talk.

'We owned pubs you know, me and Josie.'

'Did you,' said Loaf, glad to hear the conversation moving in a direction he could relate to.

'We did. We had The Irishman in Derry for years. And then when we moved back here we opened The Hook, Line and Sinker.'

'Hold on, did you say you had a bar in Derry,' asked Loaf, moving forward in his chair and shifting himself so he could look at Magnus directly.

'On William Street. That's where Josie was from.'

'You're kidding me. Derry is about a 30 minute drive from Ballyrush, my hometown.'

'I thought by your accent you were from that neck of the woods. There you go, small world eh,' came the smiling reply.

The noise from the birthday party faded away as Magnus launched into how, as a much younger man, he had worked on fishing boats which regularly sailed up the River Foyle and into Derry.

The crew would spend the night in the city, enjoying its bars and other nocturnal attractions.

It was on one of these trips that he had met Josie Gillespie working in The Irishman. Her father owned the pub and the family – Josie's parents and her sister Winnie - lived upstairs in a small two bedroom flat.

The relationship started out as infrequent four or five times a year meet ups, the two of them going to a local dancehall together or just holding hands while walking around the city's historic walls.

Eventually though they came to realise they were in love with each other. One day Magnus paid a surprise visit to Josie's father Myles and her mother Biddie to let them know he intended to ask her to marry him.

Impressed by the gentlemanly gesture, they gave him the go ahead.

'After we married we moved in with her family. But that was never going to work so we found a place of our own on Strand Road. I gave up the boats and started working full-time in the bar.

'The Irishman was a really good going place at that time, one of the busiest pubs in Derry in fact.

'It was all new to me but I loved it and I loved the city. Eventually it became too much for Myles and he handed the reins to me and Josie.

'When Myles passed away we took it on properly, just the two of us, and we ran it for over 20 years. I gave the best years of my life to that place.'

'What happened that you gave it up,' asked an intrigued Loaf.

'The Troubles happened. We knew things were going to explode, you could feel it in the air and on the streets. It was all our customers chatted about, about how something had to give.

'We were there during the Battle of the Bogside and then three years later during Bloody Sunday. What a day that was, all those poor innocent souls shot dead. Things changed after Bloody Sunday, the people changed, the city changed, Northern Ireland changed.'

He was right, the place was never the same after the events of January 30 1972. Thirteen unarmed civilians massacred by British soldiers in an episode that would echo forever through Irish society and politics.

'It was obvious that the situation was only going in one direction, all-out war. And me with this accent, we decided it was too dangerous to stay. So we sold up and moved over here. Not that there was a long queue of buyers looking for a pub in Derry in the early 1970s. But an offer did eventually come. We took it and left.'

Loaf shook his head in disbelief. How many times had he walked along William Street? How often had he been down Strand Road, usually popping in somewhere for a pint or two?

Magnus explained that on moving to the Isle of Man they settled in the quiet fishing port town of Peel.

'At first Josie struggled with the sedate pace of life but gradually came to love it.'

With the money from the sale of The Irishman, they took over The Hook, Line and Sinker in Peel which they ran until Josie fell ill.

'Motor Neurone Disease,' he revealed. 'It started with a pain in her foot. We were both working one day when she started to complain about this ache. When it wouldn't go away she went to her doctor. Nineteen months she got, nineteen short months,' he said with a shake of his head. 'She was in a wheelchair at the end, unable to speak. It was dreadful to watch, such an awful illness.'

Following her death, Magnus and his sister-in-law Winnie scattered Josie Quayle's ashes in the sea off Peel.

'It was what she wanted. I had a bench installed in her memory on the seafront there. I still get the bus up every now and then, just to say hello and to let her know I'm doing okay. It has been a long time Shaun but I see her yet, standing out there on the pier, smiling back at me. My Josie,' he said sadly.

Neither of them had noticed anyone leaving but the room was almost empty now, everyone gone for their afternoon nap. They were the only two left apart from a cleaner who was sweeping up.

'With all our talking I've missed my own party. Oh well, if God spares me I'll have another one next year.'

'Did you ever get back to Derry after you left,' asked Loaf, keen to hear how things worked out.

'I never did. Josie would go quite often to see her sister but I would always stay to look after the pub. When she died I decided I would never go back. To be honest, I couldn't face it on my own. Anytime I was there she was by my side. It didn't feel right to be going alone. Now the years have gotten the better of me and any notion of travelling is long gone.'

'And what happened to The Hook, Line and Sinker?'

'When Josie died I decided to pack it in. A developer came along and made me an offer that was far above market value. I nearly took the arm off him.'

'And how did you end up in here? I hope you don't mind me saying but I don't like it very much.'

'What do you mean how did I end up in here?'

'I mean who put you in here?'

'Put me in here,' asked Magnus with a frown that was half confusion and half schoolteacher scowl. 'It's not a prison Shaun. I put me in here.'

He got up and walked over to the kettle to make two fresh cups of tea.

'When Josie died I found myself kicking about the house in Peel on my own. But everything - every room, every smell, every ornament, every flower in the garden - it reminded me of her.

'I couldn't cope and I collapsed into the darkest place, I mean coal mine black, the deepest depression imaginable. In my mind I had nothing left to live for and I was thinking about ending it all, that taking my own life would somehow bring us together again. But I also knew how disappointed she would have been in me because she loved life so much. I honestly believe that it was her who gave me the strength to pull myself together. I went and spoke to my GP, Dr Mulligan, and she got me the help I needed. She also put me in touch with this place. A month later I packed up all my things, put the house up for rent and moved in here.'

Loaf couldn't believe that someone would live in such a facility by choice. It was literally his idea of hell. But it was also home for Magnus and many others like him.

'I don't actually live in this building, I have my own chalet out the back. It's private and no one bothers me. It can get a bit loud in here in the evenings, lots of wailing and banging and residents whose minds aren't what they once were.'

'Like Mrs Hampton.'

'You met Dora did you? She used to be the head postmistress for all of the Isle of Man you know. A really lovely woman she was too. The years haven't been kind to her unfortunately and now… well you've seen how she is.

'When it gets like that in the evenings I just head off, lock my door and do my own thing.

'I pay to live here and they look after me very well. I get all my meals cooked for me, I get my washing and ironing done and any medicines or tablets I need, there's usually a doctor not too far away. I can come and go as I please and as for the money to pay for it all, the rent from the house covers that.

'It's a good arrangement and I think Josie would approve.'

Looking at the slight, well spoken, still sharp as a whip gentleman before him in his dapper bowtie, his moustache neatly trimmed and his hair freshly cut and combed, Loaf agreed the Derry woman would be proud of her husband.

It had been a revealing afternoon and a thoroughly enjoyable one. But it was getting near time to go. Getting up from his chair, Loaf's mind looked back to a few months earlier when he'd first heard that voice, that mysterious voice asking him who he was.

It brought a smile to his lips. Life is a funny thing, he thought as he reached over to get his jacket.

'I hope I didn't bore you with all my squawking,' said Magnus. 'I wasn't planning on telling you all that, it just sort of came out.'

'I've had a lovely time and thank you for inviting me. Happy birthday again,' said Loaf, producing from his inside pocket a card and a box of Quality Street.

'Thank you for coming Shaun, it was very good of you. Now you need to go or you'll miss your bus home,' he smiled, holding out his hand for shaking.

'Take care. And I'll see you over the hedge,' Loaf called as he set off on the shortest journey home from a party he had ever made.

Chapter Twelve

The next time he walked into the library it wasn't Shanice behind the desk but Malcolm who asked him if he was member.

From his back pocket Loaf produced his form, neatly folded and tidily filled in. He handed it over like a proud schoolboy presenting his report to his parents.

'Great. Go on up and when you're finished I'll have your card ready for you to collect.'

Malcolm. Could there be a more appropriate name for a librarian, he thought as he started up the stairs.

Unlike before when it was practically standing room only, the technology suite was completely deserted.

He looked around and settled upon a computer at the far end beside the wall. It was bigger than the others which he hoped meant it would be faster, smarter even.

He rubbed his hands nervously before logging on. Had Abbey responded? What if they all had, what would he do then?

Briefly he struggled to remember his Facebook password. Then it came to him and he typed it in, using one finger at a time to avoid making a mistake.

He nibbled on his thumb as the cogs inside the machine turned. At one point the blowing sound coming from the back of it got so loud he wondered if it might take off.

The screen flashed a momentary blue before landing on his page. And there it was.

Up in the corner was the familiar red symbol indicating that he had two messages.

The first was from his sister. It was a video of a dancing duck and nothing else.

Naomi was putting her time at college to good use he thought as he quickly typed in 'That's a quacker, ha ha,' and sent it to her.

The second message had to be more interesting. He clicked on it with no clue as to what to expect.

'The Isle of Man? Does that imply the existence of an Isle of Woman,' read the rather cryptic text.

He hovered over the sender's name and pressed on the mouse.

According to her profile she was Abbey Vincent, 28-years-old from Saint John in Canada. Her occupation stated that she was an art student and a barmaid. The photo was that of the cartoon character Lisa Simpson.

It had to be his Abbey Vincent. But then again, why would the Abbey Vincent he knew write something so strange?

He thought for a minute about what his reply should be. He decided to play along.

'No Isle of Woman that I know of. There is an Isle of Dogs but I'm not sure where it is.'

Send.

He watched and listened as the icon bobbed up and down, telling him that an answer was being concocted at the other end.

'So men have their own island, dogs have their own island but us women get nothing. Quelle surprise:),' she wrote back.

He wasn't sure what the colon and single bracket punctuation meant. He Googled it to find it. It was a smiley face, albeit on its side.

He liked this conversation.

'So I'm guessing you're not the Abbey Vincent who worked with me in The Thirsty Sailor then.'

'Not that I know of, no. But I did work in an Irish bar here in Saint John up until recently.'

'An Irish bar? Are there many Irish people where you live?'

'A few. But not many. The pub is called Fáilte.'

'Fáilte, Irish for welcome,' Loaf stated authoritatively.

'I know that. And I know it's pronounced fall-cha. But a lot of the customers who come in call it fail-t which irritates the crap out of me.'

'Yeah, that would be annoying. Do they have Guinness in Fáilte?'

'Of course they do. It's not a huge seller though. Molson would be the most popular.'

'I've never come across Molson,' he wrote back. 'You said you worked there until recently. Any particular reason you left,' he asked, the conversation between them flowing.

Where every other response had been immediate, as if they were sitting across from each other, now there was a pause.

He waited for about two minutes and was just about to ask if she was still there when a response popped up.

'I have to go,' she wrote. 'But it's been nice chatting to you. I hope you find your Abbey Vincent and you two live happily ever after.'

With that she was gone.

He sat there, slightly stunned. All he had asked was why she had jacked her job in.

He scrolled back through the chat. He had learnt quite a bit about her in a matter of minutes. But he wasn't finished. He wanted to know more.

In a bit of a gloom, he thought about who else he could 'friend request' now that he was online.

Into the search bar he typed 'Evelyn Duncan Ballyrush'.

His heart fluttered as her face appeared on the screen. There she was, the first and only woman he had ever truly loved.

They had been kids really, him 19, her just turning 18. But they both felt it was the real thing.

They had met at the karate class he had taken briefly, the two of them paired up to spar on account of them being similar heights.

Afterwards Loaf had asked her if she fancied going for an ice cream.

Two Cornettos had turned into two years. Two years of going out, of going on holidays together, of talking about spending the rest of their lives together.

Until one night Loaf got drunk and smashed their happiness into a million pieces.

He was working in The Top of the Town at the time. It was a Sunday night and he finished up at 6pm, the intention being that he would collect Evelyn and take her for a meal.

Just as he was about to walk out the door he was hauled backwards by his friends' demands that he stay on for a beer.

By 11pm there was only four of them left, the rest all having faded away because of work or college the next day. There was him, his mate Stuart, Stuart's girlfriend Mandy and her pal Cora.

In sobriety he wouldn't have looked in Cora's direction. Not because she wasn't pretty but because he was head over heels about the girl who at that precise moment was at home breaking her heart, imagining he was doing exactly what he was about to do.

When he awoke the next morning with Cora beside him, he knew he had fucked up. And not just a little bit either.

His mother met them on the stairs. The stony look on her face told him she was not just furious but ashamed of him as well.

After seeing Cora off he crept back into bed and pulled the duvet over his head in the dim hope that when he awoke his world would be right again.

It wasn't and it never would be.

'You tell her or I'll tell her because there's no way I'm having a lovely wee girl like that finding out from one of the gossips in this town,' his mother scowled as she put on her coat to go out.

At first he did what all guilty men do, he overcompensated. He bought her chocolates when he never bought her chocolates. He told her was booking a foreign holiday and that he would pay for the lot.

She knew. He could tell by the way she was behaving with him that she knew. But still he denied it when she asked him out straight.

It was the following Thursday before he finally admitted that he'd spent the night with Cora. They were sitting on a bench by Moor Lake when he told her.

He couldn't look at her when he said it. But when he did there were no tears, no screams, no tantrums. Instead she met the admission in her own calm and classy Evelyn way.

She smiled gently at him, rubbed his back and said two words before walking away from him forever.

'Goodbye Shaun.'

Evelyn Duncan, his sparring partner, the woman he wanted to marry and have children with, never spoke to him again.

Eight months later she moved to Brisbane to take up a job as a care assistant.

Loaf had never gotten over her and he would regret that night, that stupid drunken stupid stupid night, for the rest of his days.

Douglas library felt like a very lonely place as he gazed at her photo. Alongside her was her husband and their two beautiful children.

She looked so happy.

He thought about pressing send on the friend request. In the end he decided against it.

She deserved better then and she deserved better now.

THE Harrison arrangement was going okay.

Every Sunday night Andy would be standing at the end of the bar. Once the pub emptied of customers Johnny or Loaf would hand him a white sealed envelope.

They weren't in any way crazy about the deal, handing over £500 to a bully who had done shit all to earn it. But neither could they risk one or both of them being dragged into an alleyway and beaten half to death or worse.

They could shoulder the burden, for now.

The drugs were more problematic than the protection money.

While enjoying a pint in The Greyhound one evening Loaf overheard a staff member chatting to a customer. While she didn't mention The Thirsty Sailor by name, it was obvious where they were discussing.

The 'bar at the bottom of Broadway' was 'full of cocaine' apparently.

They weren't far wrong. Andy and two associates – Graham and Ray - were doing the bare minimum to disguise their dealings. It was not unusual to see a customer, usually a young man or woman in their early twenties, openly flaunting the purchase they had just made.

'This is not going to end well,' Loaf hissed to Johnny one night after watching a guy literally sniff a line off the back of his mobile phone in full view of other punters.

'I know,' replied Johnny sullenly. 'I'll have a word again.'

Loaf watched him call Andy into the back room. While he couldn't hear the conversation over the Saturday night hubbub, he got the gist of it from the scornful look and laughter on Andy's face.

'How did that go,' he asked on Johnny's return.

'Brilliantly. How do you think it went,' was his cousin's sour reply as one of Andy's coked up pals knocked over a tableful of glasses on his way to the bathroom.

'Request another meeting with Charlie Harrison. I'll go with you this time.'

'Will you? Because if this continues we'll be in the ditch before the rubber has hit the road. And I can't afford to lose it Shaun, every penny I have is here, inside these four walls.'

'Of course I'll come with you. Set up a meeting and we'll try and appeal to his better nature.'

'I'm not sure he has one. But we'll give it a go,' said Johnny, lifting his phone and going out the back to send a text message.

Chapter Thirteen

July and August were relentlessly busy.

Every day was like a Saturday night with thirsty holidaymakers stopping off for a cool drink on their way up and down the promenade.

Loaf was outside The Thirsty Sailor enjoying a coffee. It wasn't yet 10am on a Friday morning and the strip was already humming with walkers, runners, sightseers and people on their way to work.

It was shaping up to be another scorcher at the tail end of a week when temperatures had rarely dipped below 25 degrees.

There was still an hour and more to start time but he had deliberately come down early to open the windows and let in some fresh air. He also wanted to spend a bit of a time by the sea before launching into a split shift – 11am to 6pm and 9pm to close.

From the wooden picnic table he was sat at he watched the waves lapping lightly at the shore. Beyond it the Irish Sea was glass-like, barely a ripple as far as the eye could see.

From behind his sunglasses he watched a jogger who was making her way along the footpath. She was wearing a tight-fitting t-shirt that read 'I Ran Man', an indication that this wasn't her first outing.

As she darted past he nodded in admiration of both her figure and her fitness. But mostly of her figure.

His impious thoughts were interrupted by a giant seagull that decided to perch itself on the edge of the table. It stared at him fearlessly, cocking its head to one side as if to tell him he was in its seat.

'Shoo,' said Loaf, worried that the bird might suddenly lunge and pluck an eye out of his head. Its beak, which was bright yellow and a good two inches in length, looked like it could do serious damage.

His shooing had little impact and the gull sat where it was for another few moments before plopping on to the ground and sauntering off to find someone more interesting to interrogate.

Loaf knitted his fingers behind his head and looked up and down the prom. The Tower of Refuge like a painting, the sea terminal glinting in the distance.

On a cloudless Friday like this, Douglas promenade was a pretty perfect place to be.

On the horizon line he could just make out a ship. It was tiny but from what he could tell, it was a cruise liner.

I wonder what the people onboard are doing, he mused to himself.

A sharp painful flick of his ear snapped him out of his daydream.

'Shit Johnny, you nearly gave me a heart attack,' he barked.

'You'll survive. What are you doing sitting here on your own anyway?'

'Just enjoying some peace and quiet before the working day begins. I was actually wondering about the people out there on that ship and what they are thinking about right now.'

Johnny had already gone into the bar. But he threw his voice back with a typically blunt reply attached to it.

'Food. I'll guarantee they're all thinking about food. It's all anyone thinks about. Speaking of which, I'm starving. Do you want anything from the café, I'm going to get a breakfast baguette.'

'I'll pass but thank you,' said Loaf, getting up from the table.

'I'll be ten minutes,' said Johnny heading off to fetch his first highly nutritious meal of the day.

Little had changed since their decision to request a second meeting with Charlie Harrison. Johnny had text him, only to receive a reply that he was out of the country. The situation regarding the antics of Andy and his goons was explained to him and he said he would have a word.

He must have done so because they were exercising a little more discretion when it came to selling their drugs. But the trade continued, much to Loaf's annoyance. Less irritated was his cousin who had begun to recognise that it brought young customers in. Alcopops were profitable and they had become The Thirsty Sailor's biggest seller. According to Johnny if anyone asked about the drugs, the staff just had to say they had no idea it was happening.

'It's nothing to do with us, do you hear me,' he had told the team. 'We see nothing, we know nothing about it. We're just innocent bar staff, serving drinks and getting on with things. Okay?'

There was still a while to go before opening. Loaf decided to pop into the back room and boot up the recently installed computer. Johnny had bought it with the grand plan that he would use it to monitor stock and keep an eye on the bar's finances. Of course it didn't quite work out that way.

After plugging it in Johnny turned to his cousin with a scratch of his gradually balding head.

'Do you know anything about this contraption? I haven't a clue.'

Using the knowledge he'd picked up during a course at Ballyrush Technical College, Loaf managed to set up a spreadsheet which had turned out to be surprisingly useful. On a Monday morning he would go through the till rolls and input the data. It would tell him what stock they had sold and what they needed to buy in.

Johnny used it for nothing other than to check Facebook. Which was what his cousin was about to do.

He had logged in a few times in the hope that the new Abbey Vincent might have contacted him again. He had given up any hope of finding the original Abbey. The picture of Evelyn and the family he didn't know she had, it had made him reconsider things.

Secretly he had always harboured hopes that they might one day reconcile. That like some smalltown love story Eveyln might return from Australia and realise that it was him, that it was only ever going to be him.

But seeing her with her boyfriend, husband, whatever he was, and their two kids, it had caught him like a right hook. She was never coming back to him.

Pining for Abbey Vincent was ridiculous. She hadn't exactly been subtle about what their night together had meant to her.

'That's so cute. But it was just sex Shaun.'

That chapter was over. Time to move on.

He fired up the computer, expecting any messages to be from his sister who had taken to sending him silly videos of penguins falling over or puppies, also falling over.

He now had 18 Facebook friends, having sought out various pals from back home. He had even managed to upload a photograph of himself, thanks to Malcolm the librarian who had actually turned out to be really helpful. Malcolm was number 18 on his list of Facebook friends.

He had mail. His heart skipped a beat when he saw that it wasn't from his sister but rather from his mysterious Canadian contact.

'What is the weather like where you are,' she asked, picking up the conversation like it had never ended.

'It's beautiful here at the moment, at least 20 degrees and it's still only early.'

'It's just coming up to 7am here in Saint John,' she replied. 'Did you manage to track down the real Abbey Vincent yet?'

'I gave up searching. I decided it was a lost cause.'

'Okay. I like your profile pic by the way, that's a very cool t-shirt you're wearing. I listened to Flogging Molly a lot when I worked in Fáilte.'

'They're a great band. Speaking of photographs, now you've seen me, let's see you,' he asked. 'Because I'm guessing that you don't look like Lisa Simpson.'

'You don't want to see a photo of me,' she said.

He did, he really did. He was just about to say so when she changed the subject.

'What are your plans for this sunny Friday?'

'I'm just about to start work here. I'm on all day unfortunately. It's really one for the beer garden.'

'Well I hope it goes smoothly. I'll check in with you again soon. Keep on the sunny side, always on the sunny side my Irish friend,' she added.

Johnny was starting to munch his way through his breakfast when Loaf emerged from the back office. His cousin already had egg down his chin and brown sauce on his t-shirt.

'I can hear your arteries clogging from here you know,' remarked Loaf on seeing the sight before him.

For a change the day started slowly. More than once they boiled the kettle and sat out front, watching the horse-drawn trams trotting their way up and down the prom.

It was coming up to 1pm when their first customer strolled in. She was in her early twenties, blonde and trendy – Nike trainers, denim shorts and a crop top with her belly button pierced. She was wearing sunglasses which she pushed up on to her head as she approached the counter.

Johnny nearly broke an ankle throwing himself through the hatch to serve her.

'Good afternoon. What can I get you?'

'I'll just have a Diet Coke please,' she replied, flashing him a pretty smile.

'No problem at all,' he said, already making wedding plans in his head. 'And how are you this fine day?'

'I'm great. I'm just out for a dander before going up to Laxey for the day. Is the owner about by any chance?'

He was like a peacock.

'You're looking at him,' he answered proudly.

'No way. You're far too young.'

Holding out his hand, he announced, 'Johnny Donnelly, proprietor, licensee and retailer of the finest beers, wines and spirits in all of Douglas town.'

'I'm Hannah,' she said, accepting the handshake.

'What can I do for you,' asked Johnny.

'Nothing really. It's just that I haven't been in here before and I was wondering how it has been going?'

Loaf was listening while polishing glasses at the other end of the bar. It was a bit of an odd conversation. She could have asked any staff member how trade was. Why ask for the owner?

And the 'you're far too young' remark. What twenty-year-old says something like that?

If there were red flags though, Johnny wasn't seeing them. In fact he was about two minutes from signing over his life and all his worldly belongings to her.

'Can I use your bathroom,' she asked when she was about halfway through her drink.

'Of course, over there, turn right and down the stairs. Be careful though because you've already fallen from heaven today, you don't want to be falling again,' he remarked with a chuckle as she picked up her bag and made her way to the ladies.

'I think I've scored here,' he told his cousin excitedly, gesturing with his head in Hannah's direction.

Loaf doubted it. But then again maybe he had. Maybe she was just genuinely interested in him. Apart from, well apart from lots of things, Johnny wasn't a bad spud.

'It does look promising although you might want to wind it in a bit. Take it easy, give her your number and see if she's about over the next week or two. Take her to that steakhouse around the corner.'

'That's a good plan Shaun. You know this, I never thought I'd say it but for once everything is coming up Donnelly.'

When Hannah returned she started preparing to leave. Johnny tore off a piece of till roll and wrote his phone number down on it. He handed it to her and suggested she call or text him.

Pulling her sunglasses out of her hair, she looked at the name and number with a nod.

'And do you have an email address,' she asked.

It was another question Loaf found slightly strange. But again he said nothing, watching instead his cousin who had hearts in his eyes and a bulge in his trousers.

'Of course,' said Johnny, scoring it down and explaining that if she was free some evening, he would like to take her out for dinner.

'I would like that very much Johnny. I'll be in touch. Have a lovely day guys,' she waved as she left.

As soon as she was out of earshot Johnny balled his fists and threw them in the air like a victorious boxer.

'YESSSSSSSS!!!!!'

Loaf looked at him bemused.

'No bother to you stud muffin. The weekend hasn't even started and you're on a promise.'

'What can I say. When you've got it, you've got it,' Johnny replied with an exaggerated strut just as Two Tellies Morrison came through the door carrying a box marked 'Hugo Ross Aftershave'.

Dropping his voice so Two Tellies wouldn't hear him, Johnny whispered, 'You look after this turnip, I'll look after the good looking ones.'

Chapter Fourteen

Magnus had fallen and broken a hip.

Loaf only became aware of the mishap when he went to the home to ask if he was okay. He hadn't been at his lookout station in the garden for almost a fortnight which was unheard of.

Concerned for his friend's wellbeing, he made the short trip around and met a nurse who was getting out of her car.

She told him that due to confidentiality, she couldn't disclose what had happened. She did confirm that he had spent five days in hospital but was now back in Sunny View and on the mend.

He was annoyed that he hadn't been informed but then again, who was going to tell him? He was just the guy who lived in the house next door, hardly immediate family.

Magnus was in the common room when Loaf got to see him. His leg was in bandage and his elbow was strapped up where he had gone down on it. He looked frail and tired in the big armchair he was sat in. But his face brightened into a huge grin when he saw who was coming through the door.

'I'm fine,' he reassured over a cup of tea. 'It was just a trip. These things happen when you're 85 Shaun. If you live to see it, you'll know what I'm talking about. Getting old is the least fun a person will ever have. Nothing gets better, everything gets worse. Things hurt, things break, some things just stop working altogether. When it happens to a car they dump it on the scrap heap or feed it into one of those big crushing machines. Us, we just have to sit here and endure it. Purgatory that's what this is, Purgatory.'

'I'm glad to hear you're in such good spirits,' Loaf replied, drawing a smile from the 85-year-old.

'I know. It's just I've been stuck here for days. I'd be ready for the madhouse if I wasn't already in it.'

'Can I get you anything,' asked Loaf.

'I'll tell you what you can do, you can help me out to the garden so I can get a smoke. In here they frown at the one thing I still enjoy. Imagine, depriving a man of my years the little happiness he still has. Here, give me a hand up.'

They spent the next hour chatting, Magnus puffing on one cigarillo after another until Loaf was sure he was going to make himself sick.

'That'll hold me for a while,' said the pensioner contentedly, mashing his fifth butt out into the ashtray.

After getting him back inside, Loaf told him he had to go.

'Already? Okay. But call again please Shaun, I don't get many visitors as you know.'

'I will of course. And you'll be back looking over that hedge, winding people up before you know it. Take care Magnus, I'll see you soon.'

He felt slightly guilty about leaving because the truth was he could have stayed. But at the same time it was his first Sunday off in months and he planned to get rolling drunk.

After going back to the flat to put on a decent shirt and a fresh pair of jeans, he headed out.

His first drink was in The Castle Tavern. He passed it practically every day but had never ventured in.

It was nice if a bit outdated. It had a carpeted floor which looked like it would be an absolute bastard to vacuum. As in so many Manx pubs there was motorcycle paraphernalia, including a helmet signed by British road racing legend Mike Hailwood. The helmet was enclosed in a Perspex box which sat on a wooden plinth. Accompanying it was a caption that explained how Hailwood had dominated the 1960s, winning multiple races and titles.

Loaf dropped a couple of quid into the fruit machine and watched his money diminish with each passing spin.

When it was gone, he drained his glass, thanked the barwoman and left.

His next stop was along the quay. The Tinker's Tavern was also a bit ramshackle and it didn't smell great. On the upside a pint was only £1.73 and it had a jukebox.

He played a couple of Springsteen tunes which seemed to go down well with the place's only other customer – a ruddy faced gentleman with a nose that was nearly purple. Loaf surmised that the reason for its colour was likely related to the manner in which he was necking large brandies on a Sunday afternoon. He knew it was time to move on when purple nose started to quiz him about the famine and why so many Irish people starved when they lived on an island that was surrounded by an ocean teeming with food.

From The Tinker's Tavern he began to make his way up through Douglas town, acquainting himself with one bar after another.

By early evening he was well sozzled but in good humour.

As he neared The Thirsty Sailor he leaned on the railings that separated the prom from the beach. It was mid-September and there was an autumn chill on the gentle breeze that was blowing up the strand.

It had been quite the summer, he thought as he raked over the events of the past months.

Original Abbey was becoming a memory. The hurt she had caused him had gradually become a reason to smile. She had made him realise that things didn't always have to be deep and meaningful, that there was a place in the world for the odd casual encounter too. Their moment together had matured him and he was glad it had happened.

And of course she had inadvertently set him on a collision course with the new Abbey Vincent with whom he conversed regularly now. Who knew where that was going to end up.

He had met Magnus who, despite an age gap of 50 years and more, had become a firm friend.

The thing with Charlie Harrison had brought them little hassle despite their initial fears that it could spell the end for The Thirsty Sailor before it had even begun.

The strippers during TT week. What the hell Johnny, he laughed, thinking back to the look on Michael's face when Pandora threw her leg up on to the bar counter, her wearing nothing but a smile and an ankle bracelet.

And, unbelievably, Johnny had been out on a couple of dates with Hannah, the crop top blonde who had strolled in off the street one sunny Friday afternoon.

It had been quite the summer, he said again as he stretched his arms out before making his way towards the bar.

How would he cope with a Manx winter which by all accounts tended to be long, dark and harsh?

We'll worry about it when the time comes, he told himself as he pushed open the door and sat himself down at the counter.

With a fresh pint in front of him, he thought back to what Johnny had said about 'everything coming up Donnelly'.

On a day like today, life certainly felt good.

SEPTEMBER 25 was his mum's birthday.

Days earlier he had popped a card in the post along with £30.

It was still only 7am when he rang her but he knew she would be up and about. Like himself, she was a morning person.

They chatted, her filling him in on all the scandal back in Ballyrush – who had been arrested, who was pregnant, what shops had opened up or closed down, who had won what at the bingo.

As she was speaking, the day's mail dropped through the letterbox. Mobile phone in one hand, she bent down and scooped up the small pile of envelopes with the other.

'You didn't have to do that son,' she said on discovering the card and money inside. 'But thank you, I was looking at a lovely dress in Harkin's the other day too. I'll go down and treat myself later on.'

'Just you do that. And I'll see you before Christmas, I promise. Have a lovely birthday mum.'

After hanging up, he started to get ready to go for a jog.

He was actually on the toilet enjoying a pre-run crap when the doorbell started ringing.

He looked at his watch. It was 7.53am.

Apart from the cops who knocks on someone's door before 8am he frowned, reaching for the loo roll.

Buzz. Buzz. Buzzzzzzzzzzzz.

'For fuck sake, hang on,' he scowled again, pulling up his pants.

Hurrying over to the window to see who was making the racket, he was met with the sight of his cousin frantically jumping and down while pointing at a newspaper.

'I'll be down now,' he shouted.

When he opened the front door it was like he had let a hurricane in.

Johnny rushed past him, spilling out garbled sentences that were heavily punctuated with 'fuck', 'bitch' and 'bastards'.

After closing the door to apartment number three, Loaf asked him to calm down and tell him what had happened.

Breathing heavily, his face like a big sweaty furious tomato, Johnny held up The Manx Recorder.

'This happened,' he shouted.

Loaf took it from him. Splashed across the front page was a picture of The Thirsty Sailor with the headline 'VODKA AND COKE: CRIME GANG USING PUBS TO DEAL DRUGS'.

'What the heck is this,' he asked, a sense of alarm rising in his stomach.

'Look. Look who it is,' said Johnny, violently poking the byline photograph of the person who had written the story.

It was her, it was Hannah Asher, the woman Johnny had been courting.

They looked at each other in disbelief.

'A journalist,' said Loaf.

Johnny couldn't find the words. He just nodded.

Loaf ran his fingers through his hair, the panic bells getting louder and louder.

'What did you tell her Johnny.'

He didn't have to wait for an answer. The look said it all.

'You told her everything. You told her about the protection money and the drugs didn't you?'

'Not the protection money, I swear I didn't mention that. But you don't understand Shaun, she told me things too. About how she had to get her wee dog put down three months ago and about how her grandad is planning on doing a skydive for his 75th birthday. We shared things Shaun.'

'Skydiving grandparents and sick puppies will not get you ten years in a Manx prison Johnny. Cocaine most certainly will. Tell me you didn't mention any names. Please tell me you didn't say who…'

Before he could get the rest of the sentence out Johnny's phone started to ring.

His hand shaking, he fished it from his pocket.

He looked at it and showed it to Loaf. It was Charlie Harrison calling.

'Don't answer,' said Loaf, his heart and his head pounding. 'Let it ring out. We need to get a read of this story first. We need to know how much damage has been done.'

They opened the paper to the two-page spread inside and laid it out on the coffee table.

The story was written in the first person and explained how Hannah Asher had decided to investigate following a reported surge in cocaine use across the island. Figures from the police and from the Department of Health showed how the number of people, particularly young people, seeking treatment for addiction had soared to an all-time high.

Asher explained that rather than just publish the statistics, she wanted to 'get behind the numbers' and find out just how bad things had become.

She revealed how over a period of two weekends she had gone from bar to bar and nightclub to nightclub, taking swab samples in each of the toilets for traces of narcotics.

These had then been sent to a laboratory for testing. Of the 18 venues she had visited, 15 showed positive readings for drugs. The highest reading by a mile was The Thirsty Sailor.

'According to scientists the readings showed that cocaine is being consumed often and in large amounts in the popular seafront bar,' she wrote.

Asher said her 'sources' had informed her that an island crime gang was forcing hospitality business owners to turn a blind eye while drugs were sold on their premises.

'In The Thirsty Sailor I watched a dealer openly hand a bag of white powder to a customer,' wrote Asher, alongside a photograph of the transaction being made.

It was a nightmare.

A line at the end of the story caused Loaf to glare at his cousin.

'All the findings in this article were provided in detail to the bar's owner, Irish national Jonathan Donnelly. He was contacted on several occasions but at the time of going to press no response had been received. All evidence has now been passed to the police.'

'Johnny...,' said Loaf with a roll of thunder in his voice.

'She never told me she was a reporter or that she was doing a story, I swear.'

'She didn't tell you about any of this at any point, not in person, not over the phone, not by text or in an email?'

'Well she might have mentioned it but...'

'But what?'

'But I wasn't really paying attention to what she was saying a lot of the time. She has both nipples pierced, did you know that?'

Loaf looked like he was going to tear his cousin into little pieces.

'Let's go back to the start. Did she tell you she was a journalist?'

Johnny took a deep breath.

'She might have said something about working for a newspaper, yes,' he admitted meekly.

'And did she say she was doing a story about drugs and crime?'

'Possibly, I can't honestly remember. Three tattoos. Did you know she has three tattoos – one on her back, one on her ankle and one somewhere very private. I didn't get to see it but another couple of dates and I...'

'Shut up about her piercings and tattoos,' shouted Loaf. 'Do you realise how much shit we're in here?'

'I know, I know, I should have worked it out, I should have paid more attention. But those piercings man, I was hypnotised by them…'

'We're screwed. The cops are going to be all over us. Is there anything in the bar I should know about, anything you and your best mate Andy might have stashed without my knowledge?'

'No no, nothing like that. Although…'

'Sweet mother of all that is holy, what now Johnny?'

'Andy was in the other night, Sunday night, envelope night. He got a bit drunk and asked if he could leave that green holdall he always has with him behind the bar.'

'What's in it?'

'I've no idea.'

'Of course you've no idea. You couldn't spot an undercover journalist when she was sitting in front of you taking notes. How could you possibly work out what a drug dealer has in a suspicious looking holdall?'

Shaking his head in disbelief, Loaf realised it was up to him to take charge.

'Okay. Here's what we'll do. We'll stay closed for a day or two and see if we can get ahead of this. I knew she wasn't right, I knew something was off that first day she came in and you chatted her up.'

'I thought she loved me,' said Johnny, a heartbroken look on his face.

In no mood for pity, Loaf snapped back, 'I wonder does the Isle of Man have a circus. Because you Johnny are one clown.'

Chapter Fifteen

They half expected the police to be waiting for them outside The Thirsty Sailor.

On their way down towards town they agreed that adopting the old hometown motto of 'whatever you say, say nothing' was the best strategy for the immediate future.

As they turned the corner at the bottom of Broadway they were greeted by…nothing. No flashing blue lights, no cordon, no warrants, no television cameras.

It was like any other day, right down to the binmen lifting the rubbish and the tractor drivers on the beach clearing the foul-smelling seaweed.

They looked at each other, relief dripping from their pores having worked themselves into a near frenzy about what might happen next.

With a trembling hand, Johnny jammed the key in the front door and let them both in.

Before he had even turned on the lights, Loaf headed straight for Andy's holdall.

He unzipped it, anticipating packages of cocaine, the kind seen in movies where the detective pulls out a pocket-knife, slices one open before rubbing the powder into his gums and declaring it to be the real deal.

Rummaging through, he found it to contain nothing but workman's tools, including a spirit level, a lump hammer and a drill.

Maybe Andy had a day job that didn't involve flogging Columbian marching powder, he thought to himself before deciding that the tools were probably a front for his nefarious trade. He could easily pass for a labourer should an inquisitive police officer pull him over.

A thorough search told him there were definitely no drugs in the bag. One less thing to worry about, he informed Johnny who was just setting down two cups of tea on the bar counter.

With their blood pressure levels starting to return to normal and a Kit Kat each for dunking, they started to talk.

They both agreed that they should speak to a solicitor.

If Hannah Asher's revelations did lead to a prosecution, they could lose their liquor licence. They needed someone who knew the law, who could let the police and the judiciary know that they had done nothing wrong. They were just a couple of innocent, hardworking Irish lads, dragged against their will into a dark and sinister underworld.

Their legal advisor might even suggest taking a case against The Manx Recorder for defamation. Asher had made The Thirsty Sailor sound like some crazed coke den, more suited to Tijuana's backstreets than Douglas's picturesque promenade.

But did they want the evidence she had gathered dragged out in a courtroom? With Johnny's previous brushes with the law, they both decided that a defamation suit might not be the smartest way to go.

On a more immediate level, they would give the place a thorough clean. The floors, the tables, the toilets, the shelves, the windowsills, everything would be scrubbed down, should any official turn up demanding to take swabs as Asher had done.

'I have to hand it to her, it was a smart piece of journalism,' Loaf told his cousin.

Johnny, still nursing a bruised ego and heart, was less than complimentary.

'She can go fuck herself. I hope her nipple piercings get infected and her tits turn green.'

The solicitor and the cleaning were the easy parts. The next stage was going to be tougher, telling Charlie Harrison that it was over, that The Thirsty Sailor was off-limits when it came to selling drugs.

The protection money too, there was to be no more. They had done their bit, they had paid their dues.

If The Thirsty Sailor managed to weather the storm that had been visited upon it, from now on it would be a narcotics-free, crime-free, Andy and his goon squad-free establishment.

A FEW days later they reopened as normal.

To their continued relief, there was still no sign of the police. Maybe Harrison wasn't boasting when he claimed to have them in his pocket.

Staff members Michael and Izzy had rung to say that they wouldn't be returning to work. According to Izzy her parents had forbade her from ever setting foot in the place again. Michael's reason was also understandable – he had plans to move to Australia and he didn't want anything to jeopardise his chances of securing a visa.

It was another headache that had to be navigated. But a minor one compared to what was coming up – a meeting with the Isle of Man's number one crime boss.

Following several missed calls, Johnny had eventually answered the phone to him.

'You'll come to my house,' Harrison had told him. 'Andrew will pick you up at your bar and bring you here.'

The cousins agreed to rendezvous in The Thirsty Sailor at 6pm where they would await Andy's arrival.

Loaf walked through the door to the sound of Lilly Armstrong singing at the top of her voice.

'We'll meet again

'Don't know where

'Don't know when

'But I know we'll meet again some sunny day…'

'Lilly, do you not think this place has taken enough of a battering without you adding to our woes,' he called as she brought her one-woman show to a close.

Full of Cinzano and peppermint, she either didn't hear him or didn't care. She just raised her glass and smiled in his direction.

Minutes later he was joined by Johnny who for some reason had decided to put on a shirt and tie for the engagement.

'There's nothing wrong with wanting to look smart,' he said when quizzed about his choice of clothing.

At 6.45pm a black Mercedes appeared outside. Andy beeped the horn to signal that he was ready to take them on their mystery tour.

Johnny opened the door to get into the front seat but was quickly redirected.

'In the back dumbass. Only Mr Harrison sits in the front.'

He said little else as he drove them out of Douglas, humming along instead to Erasure who were coming from the CD player.

'I tried to discover, a little something to make me sweeter…' he drummed on the steering wheel.

They stuck to the coast for 15 minutes before turning down a narrow dirt road that had grass growing up through the tarmac.

The path led them past an old derelict church that, by the look of it, hadn't welcomed a congregation in over a century.

It was the only other building on an otherwise deserted stretch.

It was starting to get dark when the track came to an end. In front of them was a brick cottage, the kind commonly found in rural Donegal. There was a light on and smoke billowing from the chimney.

Andy stopped the car, got out and knocked on the door.

In his absence his two passengers exchanged words.

'We're in the middle of bloody nowhere,' said Johnny.

'I see that,' Loaf replied in a worried tone. 'It would be a great place to bury a couple of bodies.'

As Andy was knocking for a second time, Charlie Harrison opened the door. He was wearing tracksuit bottoms, a cardigan and bedroom slippers. Tucked under his arm was a newspaper. Neither of his guests needed a degree to work out what paper it was.

Loaf, who was seeing him for the first time, agreed that there was a passing resemblance to Granda Donnelly.

'He's not exactly Don Corleone,' whispered Loaf, referring to Harrison's attire.

'And not exactly a mafia palace he's living in either,' muttered his cousin as they stepped out of the vehicle.

They both had to stoop slightly to get through the cottage's low front door.

The hallway was just about big enough for the two of them. Through a second low-framed door and they were in the living area.

The walls were white-washed brick while the floor was red tiles. There was a sofa that had seen better days, a rocking chair, a comfortable looking armchair and a coffee table. There was a television and a dresser on which sat old black and white family photographs. On one of the walls hung a Sacred Heart picture, illuminated by a glowing red candle.

Beside the open fire sat a basket of turf.

It really was straight out of Donegal, thought Johnny, breathing in the familiar earthy aroma.

'Have a seat gentlemen,' said Harrison, pointing to the sofa.

'Can I get you a cup of tea? There's a pot freshly made.'

The offer was unexpected but welcome.

'I would love a cup of tea,' replied Johnny, taken aback by the warm greeting.

'I'll have one too,' added Loaf.

'Andrew, if you don't mind,' Harrison directed his right hand man who looked none too pleased at being relegated to teaboy.

He saw them taking in the cottage and explained that it was the only place he had ever lived.

'Me, my folks, my brother and my sister all grew up in this house. My parents are long dead and I hope they're happy wherever they are. When my mother died I bought the rest of them out.

'Now it's just me, these walls and my own private beach. Every morning and every evening I'm in the sea for a dip, regardless of the weather or time of year. It's good for my hip which as you can see is a bit of a bugger.'

Andy placed a tray holding a large teapot, two mugs, milk and sugar on the table.

Harrison indicated that they help themselves. But as they were doing so he roared a sentence that sent their hearts racing.

'RIGHT ANDREW, SHOOT THE TWO OF THEM!'

Andy moved as if he were reaching for a weapon from his waistband.

'What the fuck,' screamed Johnny, spilling his tea all over his lap.

Loaf jumped to his feet ready to fight. His face was as white as the cottage's walls.

'Calm down, calm down,' shouted Harrison. 'I'm joking, I swear I'm only joking.'

Andy threw his hands in the air to show it was a hoax, that he didn't actually have a gun.

Then he broke into near hysterics.

'The look on your faces,' Andy cackled, the tears running down his cheeks. 'That was a classic.'

'Andrew get this man a towel please, he's covered in tea,' said Harrison as everyone caught their breath again.

'That was a shitty thing to do Mr Harrison,' remarked Johnny, frowning and furious that his best shirt now had a muddy brown stain down the front of it.

'That was just to remind you who's boss.'

Harrison unfolded The Manx Recorder and spread it out on the coffee table in front of him.

Sweeping his hand across the two pages of headlines, he said, 'I had it all under control - The businesses, the cops, Andrew and his team, it was all running so smoothly. Until you two royally fucked everything up.

'According to my contact inside the constabulary the chief inspector nearly hit the roof when she saw this splashed across the press. She said anyone reading it would think the criminals were running the island. She has ordered a full investigation into organised crime. Me and my men are under surveillance apparently. Plain clothes officers are being sent in to monitor the pubs and clubs. And our do-gooder politicians are to discuss an emergency bill calling for anyone caught selling drugs to be given a minimum ten years in jail.

'All because you two got a hard-on for Miss Asher here.'

Loaf wasn't loving that the episode was being treated as some sort of joint enterprise. He was completely innocent of any wrongdoing but was still being held to account for it. At the same time, he wasn't going to let his cousin carry the can on his own.

'This is costing me a fortune,' Harrison continued. 'It will be at least three months before Andrew and his team can go back to work. I'll be out of pocket to the tune of at least £250,000. Do you think that's fair Mr Donnelly and Mr Donnelly? Do you?'

His voice had an edge to it, one that tied Johnny's tongue up. Not so much Loaf though who was quietly fuming. He was annoyed not only by the question but by the injustice of the whole situation.

'Fair? No harm to you Mr Harrison, but you've a brass neck talking to us about what's fair and not fair.

'Do you think leaning on me and Johnny is fair, a couple of ordinary lads trying to run a legitimate business? Putting us in a spot where we could lose everything, where we could end up in prison even? You've a bit of a cheek, do you not think?'

Harrison said nothing for about 20 seconds. Eventually a slight smile crept across his lips.

'Maybe you're right Shaun,' he replied slowly.

It was the first time he had called him by his first name.

'Which brings us to the bigger question – what is fair? What does fair even mean? Is it fair that the British government uses taxpayers' money to buy bombs that get dropped on starving families in countries you and I would struggle to find on a map?

'Is it fair that billions of pounds of public money are being used to bail out the banks while the fat hogs laugh about it in their villas in Monaco?

'Of course not, none of it is fair. But that's the world we live in Shaun, where life is cheap and criminals get away with murder.

'I'll bet your old man grew up listening to the same bullshit as me - An honest day's work for an honest day's pay. I did my fair share of honest days and you know where they got me? Nowhere.

'Let me tell you a story – My first job was in a shoe factory. It was about ten miles from here so I needed a car to get to it. The week before I started I went out and bought myself a second-hand Cortina on credit. Then I went to work, making shoes for a geezer who would have paid us in shoelaces if he'd been allowed to. Do you know what most of my salary went on? Paying for the car I needed to get me to my work. I had to put fuel in it, I had to insure it, I had to make sure it was roadworthy. Five years it took me to pay that car off. I'll never forget the day I made my final payment. I'll never forget it because it was the day the engine packed up and I had to start all over again.

'Do you see what I'm saying? The whole system is a con. Ordinary people like me and you slogging our guts out, fighting with each other over trivial things. While those in power rake in millions, billions even, doing deals with dictators, gunrunners and diamond smugglers.

'We're down here while up there the pheasant-eating, cognac-quaffing elite are playing us like a fiddle.'

Loaf listened with interest. Having worked in bottom rung jobs most of his life, he could relate to the anecdote about the factory.

But Harrison wasn't demanding protection money from billionaires or banks or the system of which he spoke with such derision. He was standing on the fingers of his neighbours.

'It took me a long time but when I eventually copped on that government is just a posh word for organised crime I decided that I was going to take my share. If it was good enough for them then it was good enough for me.

'What I do now Shaun, it's just business, it's economics page one - supply and demand. People want drugs, I get them drugs.

'Yes I need your premises and yes I skim a little off your profit margin. But the £500 you pay me, I'm sure you make that back through the customers my narcotics bring into your pub.

'Everyone's a winner, would you not agree?'

To his surprise, by the end of the monologue Loaf found himself not in total disagreement with Charlie Harrison's point of view.

But the fact remained that he and Johnny and many others like them were being forced to bow down to the man in front of him. To Harrison £500 per week was pocket money. To the owners of The Thirsty Sailor it was over £25,000 a year.

'You may have convinced yourself that you're an ordinary, decent criminal Mr Harrison, that you're harming no one. But you are. And we want out. We came to this island to play with a straight bat, not to be bullied and made a fool of.'

Johnny sat up so he was shoulder to shoulder with his cousin. You tell him Loaf.

'You want out,' asked Harrison with an air of surprise in his voice.

'We're here to negotiate, that's all. Yes we fucked up with the Hannah Asher thing but there will be consequences for us too. All we're asking is to be left alone.'

'You have got balls Shaun, I'll give you that,' said Harrison, throwing another lump of turf on the fire and poking it around until the flames were licking up the chimney.

He stared at it for about 30 seconds before speaking again.

'Gentlemen, can you give me a couple of minutes so I can speak to Andrew. I've just had a thought which might work for all of us.'

Loaf and Johnny got up from the sofa and stepped outside.

They were glad of the cold air, a break from the tension and the blazing fire.

'Fair play to you, that took guts,' said Johnny.

'You don't ask, you don't get,' replied Shaun, feeling in no way brave or heroic. 'Let's hear what he has to say.'

Minutes later Andy opened the door to let them back in.

Charlie Harrison explained that he had a large shipment of cocaine coming in by sea in time for the Christmas rush.

'You two are going to go and get it for me,' he announced.

'You want us to bring in a shipment of drugs? What do we know about drug smuggling,' asked Loaf.

'You won't be smuggling anything. The smuggling will have been done before you get anywhere near it. All you have to do is pick it up from the pier and drive it to a safe house.'

'Why us? Why not send Andy and a couple of the hoods he hangs about with?'

'Because you two owe me. It'll be pay back for what your stupidity has cost me. But also, Andrew has to keep his head down. We're under surveillance, remember?'

The two cousins looked at each other. Johnny nodded as if he was up for it. Loaf wasn't just as ready to bend over.

'And do we get anything in return?'

'You get to keep your kneecaps, how does that sound? But also, with it being Christmas and all, I'll consider your request.'

'You'll consider leaving us to get on with our lives without any more hassle,' asked Loaf.

'I will.'

'If we're caught we're looking at serious jail time.'

'True. But life, my young friend, is a constant dance between risk and reward. Think about that. Now Mr Donnelly and Mr Donnelly, I have other things to do. Andrew here will escort you back to Douglas.'

The meeting was over. What they had was not so much an offer but an order. But it was something.

Risk and reward, just as Charlie Harrison had said.

⚜

Chapter Sixteen

It was Andy who relayed the finer details to them.

Huddled around a table one night after closing time, he explained that the drugs were worth about £8 million and were being brought from Amsterdam to Blackpool and then from Blackpool on to the island.

The surprisingly sophisticated plan involved the waterproofed packages being dropped by a 'mother ship' into the sea off Castletown in the early hours of December 2.

They would be wrapped in flotation devices equipped with trackers, enabling a crew on shore to monitor them. The land team would then take a smaller boat out and collect the shipment before bringing it back to the harbour.

'This is where you come in,' he told them. 'From Castletown pier, the packages need to be taken to a warehouse in Ramsey.'

A 40 kilometre drive through the Manx countryside in the dead of night, with freedom the prize awaiting them once it was mission complete.

It sounded simple. But the downside was terrifying. The local press was awash with horror stories of people being jailed for long spells after being nabbed with much smaller quantities of narcotics.

If by some terrible twist of fate they were caught, they were looking at 15 to 20 years in prison.

'What choice do we have,' asked Johnny as he and his cousin dashed into a coffee shop in Port St Mary to escape the downpour that had blown in out of nowhere.

They took off their dripping wet coats and sat themselves close to a radiator by the window.

'Our options are few, no doubt about it,' said Loaf in a low voice. 'We could walk away from the whole thing. We could pull the door behind us, get on the Seacat and be back in Belfast tomorrow, away from all this madness.'

'Not a chance. There's no way I'm going home with not a penny in my pocket. I'd rather set the place alight and me in it than do that. Besides, what's to say Harrison wouldn't come after us? He reckons we owe him after the Hannah Asher splash and he strikes me as the kind of man who doesn't let people walk out the door without paying.'

'There's an idea. We could burn the place and claim off the insurance.'

'It did cross my mind. There's only one problem, I don't actually have insurance yet. When I priced it, it was costing a small fortune. I said I would leave it for a year until I got some money built up.'

'That's it then. We have no choice other than to do the job,' said Loaf, ordering two sausage rolls and a mug of tea from the waitress.

'It looks like it,' Johnny agreed. 'The good news is that there's eight weeks between now and December 2. Eight weeks of peace and quiet – no Andy, no drugs.'

'Eight weeks of worry you mean.'

'There he is again, Serious Shaun. Look on the bright side, once it's done that's us, home and dry.'

'IF you were stranded on a desert island and you had to cannibalise someone to keep yourself alive, which part of them would you eat first?'

Declan 'Knickers' McKenzie's question caused Angie and Bert Russell to glance sideways at each other.

Knickers had only just walked in. After ordering a pint he had invited himself to sit down opposite them. No 'Hello' or 'How are we doing folks', just this question, asked in his deep baritone voice, which he had obviously been mulling over.

'I've no idea Declan,' replied Angie, shifting uncomfortably in her seat at the way he was looking at her. 'It's not something I've ever given much thought to.'

'What about you Bert, which part of the human anatomy would you go for first,' asked Knickers, turning his attention towards her husband.

'You're quite a strange man, has anyone ever told you that Declan? But now when you're asking, I would say the calves. The calves seem pretty meaty. And there's no bones to worry about, just tendon and muscle.'

'That's interesting. I would have said the neck myself but the calves, that's a good shout there Bert. Did you watch the football last night…'

From being Hannibal Lecter, Knickers McKenzie was suddenly a normal human being again.

Loaf had listened to the ghoulish exchange from behind the bar.

'See him there,' he whispered to new recruit Aaron, nodding in McKenzie's direction. 'You mark my words, one day you'll see that man on television, being rushed from a prison van into a courtroom with a blanket over his head.'

The new start had no idea what was going on.

'Okay,' answered Aaron with a confused and slightly frightened look on his face.

Loaf's smile quickly dissolved when he looked up to see a policeman and policewoman coming through the door.

Their appearance caused everyone in the bar to turn and stare.

Before the officers reached the bar counter Loaf slipped Aaron his phone and told him to ring Johnny.

'Tell him it's urgent.'

'Good afternoon sir, I'm Constable O'Brien, this is Constable Drury,' they introduced themselves.

This was it then, the big bust. They were going to order the place be shut down and both the owner and the manager taken into custody.

He did an admirable job of keeping his cool despite the panic that was bubbling in him.

'Yes, what can I get you,' Loaf asked as if they were two normal punters in for a quiet drink.

Constable Drury, the female half of the dynamic duo, smiled at the little joke.

'We're fine, thank you,' she replied. 'We just happened to be in the area and thought we would call in.'

Having worked in bars back home for years, Loaf knew fine well that the cops were never 'just in the area'. Never.

'We were hoping to have a quick look around, to make sure everything is as it should be,' said Constable O'Brien.

'Fill your boots. You see most of it here already, a few locals enjoying their drinks. If you want a tour of the toilets, they're down that flight of stairs there.'

The two officers spent ten minutes inspecting the main bar, even going as far as to crouch down to examine the pool table's innards via the hole where the balls came out.

When they were done with upstairs, they started down to look at the lavatories.

As they were descending, Johnny came bounding through the door.

'Where are they?'

'Downstairs checking the bogs.'

Thrusting an envelope in his cousin's direction, Johnny told him, 'I met with that solicitor this morning. Have a scan over that, a copy of it is already on its way to the chief inspector.'

Written on paper headed 'Beattie & Co Legal Services', the letter ran to a couple of pages.

'My clients have fallen victim to an unscrupulous journalist who clearly values sensationalism over truth.

'Mr Jonathan Donnelly will testify that Ms Asher used her physical appearance and implied promises of a carnal nature to illicit information from him, information that even a cursory investigation will find to be a fairytale conjured up to impress an attractive young woman.

'With regard to the photograph of drug dealing within The Thirsty Sailor licensed premises, the transaction took place without my clients' knowledge. Had they been aware, they would have put an end to the activity immediately. They have since taken steps to address the problem and are happy to walk the constabulary through these measures.

'We have also today written to The Manx Recorder to inform them that we will be seeking compensation for reputational damage.'

The thud of boots told them that Drury and O'Brien were on their way back up.

'Well officers, did you find anything,' asked Johnny.

'And who are you,' inquired Drury.

'I'm Jonathan Donnelly, owner. And this is my bar manager Shaun Donnelly. We have a good idea why you're here. Feel free to look around as much as you want, you won't find anything illegal in here.

'It's actually quite syrupdipitous that you've dropped in because I have a letter here from our solicitor, a copy of which is on its way to your boss. It lays out our position in full.'

They waited while the officers read over the pages they had been handed.

It appeared to satisfy them that the matter was being handled at a level well above their pay grade.

'Okay Mr Donnelly and Mr Donnelly, thank you for your time. We'll be seeing you again no doubt.'

'Hopefully not Constable Drury. But have a good day.'

With the officers gone, Loaf turned to Johnny.

'Syrupdipitous? Did you mean serendipitous?'

'Ah sure I was close enough. Knock that kettle on please Aaron.'

'I'm going to use the computer for half an hour if you don't mind,' Loaf told his cousin as normal service resumed around them.

'Work away.'

Chatting with Abbey Vincent had become his favourite part of the week.

They had agreed that rather than fragmented messages, written and read at random times due to the time difference, they would get together online at the same time every Thursday.

This was their third such meeting.

So far he had learnt that she was almost exactly two years younger than him, their birthdays falling just four days apart.

Her middle name was Erica and she had studied sculpture at Saint John Art Academy. She had two brothers, one of whom was Logan who had spent a year at Trinity College in Dublin.

She had a four-year-old Cockapoo named Tarantino and she could recite every line ever uttered by her favourite Friends character Phoebe Buffay.

When they were together the conversation tended to flow freely and it could be about anything - from the weather to their schooldays to the Kennedy assassination to the latest episode of Lost. And they could chat for 20 minutes or two hours, depending on availability and mood.

While neither of them said it, they both knew.

Things between them had begun to move beyond casual chatter. Their weekly catch-ups were now more like dates, each waiting nervously for the other to log on and fill them in on the latest news.

The conversations had become deeper, more personal. Abbey had even begun signing off some of her messages with an x, an addition Loaf liked very much.

Still he hadn't seen her though. Despite a number of requests for a photograph, she had repeatedly declined, always pushing back with evasive messages like 'I'm not sure you would be able to cope with my beauty' or 'My natural radiance might short circuit your computer'.

Today's long-distance discussion started with the news that Tarantino had been to the groomers and was now, officially, 'the most stunningly attractive dog in Canada and possibly the entire world'.

A photo popped up of Tarantino who appeared to be smiling proudly at his ascent to the position of king of all canines.

'Tell him woof woof, it's a thumbs up from me,' wrote Loaf, adding 'And by the way, I've seen at least a dozen photographs of your dog yet not a single one of you.'

He knew it was a touchy subject so rather than risk derailing the conversation, he quickly added, 'Anyway, never mind Tarantino, what about you, how are you doing?'

'I'm doing okay. A bit tired but nothing I can't cope with.'

'You said that last time too. Maybe you should see a doctor.'

There was a brief halt in her replying.

He didn't know why but in that moment he could sense that their relationship had reached a crunch point.

'Shaun, if I send you a photograph of me please promise you won't say something cruel. I'm not able for that right now.'

He read the message with a frown. Cruel? She was one of the funniest, most genuine people he had ever encountered. It hurt a little that she even felt it necessary to ask him such a question.

'I won't, I promise.'

As he sat there waiting, he wondered what it was she was so reluctant to reveal about herself.

He leaned back in his chair and tried to imagine what she must be thinking at that exact moment, alone in her bedroom in Saint John. There was clearly something serious troubling her.

The lull in communication allowed him to reflect on their friendship.

How mad was it that all this had been born out of error? It was like that film, Sliding Doors. Had someone else answered his message during his search for the original Abbey Vincent, their worlds would never have collided. They would have gone about their days eternally oblivious to the other's existence.

Was it fate? Did he even believe in fate, that somewhere out there a divine being was weaving the threads of human life? Or was it just a happy accident, like finding twenty quid on the walk to work or waking up feeling perfectly fresh after a heavy night on the ale?

Whichever it was, it had been a blessing. And whatever it was she was nervous about, she needn't be. He was already hooked by her wit, her intellect and her good nature. Like the way when he had joked to her about his cousin Johnny going bald. Rather than laugh along she had pointed out that it probably wasn't easy for him, a relatively young man losing his hair like that.

The gentle reprimand had made him stop and think. She was right, Johnny probably was quietly self-conscious about it. He didn't need his pal slagging him off and making him feel even worse.

Abbey Vincent was a decent person. And in an increasingly greedy, angry and self-interested world, decent people weren't just that easy to come by.

His heart jumped as his monitor sprung to life.

And there she was, Abbey Erica Vincent.

The photo's caption ran to five words…

'Shaun, I have terminal cancer'.

Chapter Seventeen

I t had started as a lump no bigger than a pea.

Abbey Vincent, then aged 22, was on a weekend away with her friends when she discovered it. They had travelled down to Toronto to celebrate Shelly's 21st, the agenda items being shots, cocktails and flirting with guys.

They were staying in the Marriott, Abbey and Deborah in room 406, Shelly and her sister Rosie next door in 407. Room 406 and that bloody wonky key card that you had to jiggle up and down to get it to work. No easy task when you were six Moosehead lagers and as many margueritas deep.

It was nearing 7pm and she was looking in the mirror while fixing her bra. Her favourite top and jeans were laid out neatly on the bed, ready to accompany her on whatever adventure the night ahead had in store.

The chill that ran through her on feeling the bead-like intrusion was something she would never forget.

Her immediate reaction was to ignore it. She was 22 for crying out loud, 22-year-olds didn't get…that.

She told no one because it was nothing. It was a cyst. It was her body changing, she was now in her twenties after all. Or it was an injury. That's what it was, it was when she had overstretched at Pilates the other week.

It would clear up, evaporate, never to be heard of or mentioned again.

Three weeks later though and it was still there. And was she imagining it or had it become more prominent?

If she hadn't been sitting down, her knees would have buckled at what Dr Rosario told her during the emergency appointment she managed to get.

'I'm going to send you for further investigation. But Abbey promise me you won't attend this next appointment on your own, that you'll take someone with you.'

It became too much to keep to herself. The following Thursday evening while helping make the dinner, she broke the devastating news to her mum Francine.

Watching someone's face fall completely, that instant emotional change, the blanket of silence that envelopes the room, it was something she would become very used to.

'I'm the world's worst superhero, Dreadful News Woman,' was her joke to try and make the situation less awful when she told her friends.

Within two weeks they – Abbey with her mum at her side - were sitting across the desk from a consultant, Dr Murthy.

Dr Murthy, or Cindy as she preferred to be called, informed them that a mammogram had already been booked.

'The younger a patient is, the thicker their breast tissue tends to be,' Cindy explained. 'It makes the cancer harder to detect. But let's get you in for a mammogram and see what it tells us.'

What was supposed to be a single biopsy became six. And the results were not good.

When they met with Dr Murthy again, she told them the various scans and tests had detected a tumour measuring ten centimetres. There would have to be an operation followed by both chemotherapy and radiotherapy.

It was time to tell the rest of the family.

Abbey gathered her father Tristan and her two brothers, Logan and Mike, around the kitchen table.

She could tell from the looks on their faces they were expecting her to announce she was pregnant.

Her father's expression was one of nervousness while her brothers smirked knowingly at each other.

Any light-hearted humour was quickly zapped when she disclosed her diagnosis.

'You should have told me,' said Tristan, banging his hand on the table and looking crossly at his wife rather than his daughter.

'I know sweetheart but it was a woman thing. And we had to wait for the test results.'

'I'm sorry too dad,' added Abbey. 'It wasn't mom's fault, I asked her not to mention it until we were sure.'

Her first surgery took place on December 11 2001. Exactly three months earlier the world had watched in horror as two planes smashed into the Twin Towers in New York.

Walking through the revolving door of Christ The King Hospital with her overnight bag on her shoulder, Abbey Vincent felt like it was her world that was crashing down around her.

'Happy Christmas Abs,' she said to herself in a low voice as she passed a cheerful Santa and two plastic reindeer on the way to the lift that would take her up to ward nine.

When the surgeons went in with their scalpels they found the ten centimetre tumour but also a second one measuring five centimetres. Apparently the little pea she had discovered was 'the tip of the iceberg'.

She would later tell Deborah, her best friend and roommate that night in the Marriott, that they 'gutted me'.

'They took 14 lymph nodes, that's how aggressive it was,' she explained over coffee.

Six weeks after surgery came the part she had been dreading more than anything - chemotherapy.

The night before her first chemo session she did something she hadn't done since she was eight-years-old and a pupil at Lancaster South School. She got down on her knees at the side of her bed and prayed that she wouldn't lose her hair.

As she had been warned it probably would be, chemo was gruelling. As tough as it was though, the steroids that went with it were worse.

They caused her to feel like the Incredible Hulk, like she could lift a car and toss it across the road if the notion took her. A second side effect was 'moon face', a swelling that made her look puffy, bloated and unnaturally round.

She felt like she was losing her grip on reality. Looking out her living room window, shaking, sweating, her heart going like a freight train due to the roid rage, she put her head in her hands and stifled a scream that had it got out, it would have had the neighbours calling the police.

'No more steroids and no more bloody moon face. I don't care what the consequences are, I'm not taking them,' she told Dr Murthy.

Despite her tearful pleas to a higher power regarding the long brown locks she loved so much, her hair began to fall out in clumps.

Initially she was too sick and weak to care. But by week three when she was starting to regain some strength, it began to hit home.

'There are things you will never know unless they happen to you,' she told her mother as she tried to articulate her hair loss ordeal into words.

'Your head is really sensitive because of the chemo and all the drugs they give you. When your hair is coming out, it's like a dragging sensation but a million times worse. Every little spike is like a needle being ripped from your scalp.'

The excruciating description brought a tear to Francine's eye. She knew how fond her daughter was of her hair. As a little girl Abbey would sit on a Saturday night as her mum gently combed it 100 times, always with her favourite brush, the one with Snow White on it. Above her bed Abbey had seven different coloured bows, one for each day of the week.

Now it was all gone, stolen by a disease that had she somehow been able, Francine would have gladly taken from her and carried herself.

All she could do was pull her daughter close and hug her tightly. Her natural instinct was to tell her it was going to be okay, that all this unpleasantness would pass eventually.

But it wouldn't. And her daughter, this smart, beautiful, logical young woman who was having to shoulder what felt like an endless cascade of horrors, would not have appreciated it.

LOAF stared at the screen for a solid five minutes.

Terminal cancer.

What did that mean?

He knew what it meant, it meant that she had cancer and that she was going to die from it.

But when? Tomorrow? The next day? Next month? Next year?

There was little in her photograph to suggest she was ill, never mind terminally.

Her face was pleasant and friendly looking. You could tell from it that she liked to laugh.

She had big dark eyes and a wide smile. Her teeth were white and straight, probably as a result of braces as a teenager. They were perfect apart from a small chip in one at the front. It made him want to find out how the blemish came about – a childhood tumble down a slide? A playground tussle with a boy that she secretly fancied? A drunken escapade?

Her hair was brown, tied back in a small ponytail.

She was wearing eight earrings, four in each ear – two gold hoops in each lower lobe and two higher up in the cartilage.

She was…she was cool, that's what she was.

But what to write? How do you respond to such a bombshell being dropped?

The chat box icon started to oscillate, indicating that a message was incoming.

'I know it's a lot to take in,' she wrote. 'And you're probably wondering what to say.'

It was exactly what he was wondering.

Before he could respond, she added, 'If it's any help, you can say 'I don't know what to say to you'. I find it refreshing when people do that, it's so much better than 'I'm sorry' or 'You poor dear'. It's better because the simple truth is that I don't know what to say either.'

Loaf breathed deeply, trying to figure out what to do.

As he sat there trying to find the words, a voice he vaguely recognised reached him from the bar.

He had to go. He needed time.

'Look Abbey, I'm at work here and I'm going to have to get back to it. We'll chat again in a few days. You're right, I don't know what to say. But I will. The next time we talk, I'll know what to say.'

He hesitated before adding a very genuine x and o – a kiss and a hug – to the end of his message.

He emerged from the back office to find six customers dotted around the place.

Seated over by the pool table rolling a cigarette was someone he hadn't seen since the ferry crossing.

Stepping through the hatch, he walked over to say hello.

'Terry, it's me, Shaun, we met on the boat over from Belfast.'

Terry, who was wearing combat trousers, steel toe-capped boots and a high viz hoodie, looked up in surprise.

A smile crept across his face as he clocked who was speaking to him.

'Oh my days. Mr Loaf.' Rising from his seat, he threw out his hand. 'How have you been?'

'I've been great Terry. What about you?'

'You know the score fella, working, drinking, drinking, working. What else is there to do really? We're flat out up at the hospital, I've been on site the last seven days in a row. But a couple of days off now will see me right.'

After pausing briefly to take a drink from his beer, he continued, 'So this is the place you were telling me about. It's nice, I like it.'

'This is it, The Thirsty Sailor. And here he is, the boss man,' Loaf announced as Johnny joined them.

'Who's this then?'

'Johnny meet Terry, I bumped into him on the ferry. It seems like ages ago now.'

'Well Terry from the ferry, welcome to The Thirsty Sailor.'

'Cheers Johnny. Although to be honest the wind didn't just blow me in here. I saw this place in the paper the other week and thought I'd pop in to see what all the fuss was about. It never occurred to me that I might find my man Loaf here. Where do you keep all the cocaine then?'

Johnny smiled.

'Don't even joke about it. What a mess.'

'Last week's news now guys. If I was you I wouldn't be getting my knickers in a knot over it. Look lads, what are you doing this evening? Do you fancy a couple of pints?'

Still reeling from Abbey's revelation, Loaf really wasn't in the form. But another time, for sure. Terry seemed like a solid sort, the kind of person he could get along with.

'Not tonight but maybe next week? Give me your number and I'll text you.'

'I'll have a pint with you,' said Johnny. 'I'm working here the rest of the evening but I can sip a few cold ones. I might even head on to Marbles afterwards, it stays open until 2am.'

After buying Terry a pint Loaf headed back to start cashing up at the end of his shift.

At 6pm he handed over the keys and put on his coat.

The streetlights were already on as he stepped out into the October shadows.

Where the last few days had been breezy, this evening the air was perfectly still.

Instead of his usual route up Broadway and through Derby Square he opted for a longer way home – down past the Villa Marina to Sam Webb's pub, then turn right on to the ridiculously steep Crellin's Hill. It was a tight climb but it would give him the chance to think.

By the time he was pushing the key into the front door of number 12 he had made his decision.

Shaun Donnelly was going home.

Chapter Eighteen

'It's only for a few days,' he told Johnny. 'I'll be back long before the 'you know what' on December 2.'

He needed time away. He needed to see his mum. He never thought he would say it but he needed the familiar streets of Ballyrush.

Following lengthy negotiations Johnny eventually agreed, albeit reluctantly.

He'd been in a mood for days, tetchy and hard to reason with. Loaf put it down to the amount of drinking he'd been doing. He and Terry had been out on the lash every night for the last week.

Terry was now a Thirsty Sailor regular. The night of his initial appearance he and Johnny had indeed ended up in Marbles. Terry knew some of the security crew who had given them permission to sit on after closing. According to Johnny it was nearly 5am before they finally fell out of the place.

Terry had returned the following evening and then the evening after that again. There was hardly a day now when he didn't call in for an after-work beer and a game of pool.

He seemed to be liked among those who frequented the pub. The only dissenting voice was Two Tellies Morrison who felt there was something 'not right' about him.

'I don't know, there's just something sneaky about him. And before you say it, no, it's not because he's Black.'

Two Tellies didn't like many people so his concerns over Terry were both noted and disregarded in the same second.

'Don't be mentioning this carry on with Harrison to anyone back in Ballyrush, do you hear me,' warned Johnny after granting his cousin his time off. 'If anyone asks, and they will ask because the town is full of nosey bastards, just you tell them that we're doing well, we're making good money and that we're already thinking of expanding the empire.'

'Expanding the empire? Jeez, calm down Richard Branson.'

'Not a word to anyone, including your mum. Because she'll tell my mum and then both our mums will know. And you know what they're like.'

'I know, I heard you the first time. My lips are sealed,' said Loaf, drawing his fingers across his lips to demonstrate that they were indeed fastened shut.

The arrangement was that he would work Halloween night before travelling to Belfast the following day. Sailings were scarce so late in the year so his journey would have to be by air.

Tomorrow was 'Abbey Day' as he had Christened it once during their conversations. His face had turned red with embarrassment when he'd disclosed the name to her but as he knew she would, she'd met it with similar affection.

'Well that must make it Shaun Day here in Saint John then! I love that. But let's not tell anyone, okay? It'll be nice to have our own little secret, don't you think?'

He'd had time to digest her cancer revelation and the more he thought about it, the less freaked out by it he had become.

They had been in contact for months now and she had never given any indication that she was unwell. Quite the contrary in fact, she had always sounded upbeat, like she was quite happy in her little corner of the world.

He had questions. Of course he had, who wouldn't in such a situation? Her illness had added a new dynamic to their relationship. But she was still the same Abbey Vincent who loved reading Stephen King novels and who had a better grasp of the complexities of Irish politics than most people.

If anything, her news had made him want to get even closer to her. He was captivated by this beautiful woman with the wide smile and multiple earrings who for a few hours each week made him feel like he was the only man in the world.

'WHAT the fuck do I do here,' Loaf muttered, staring at the broken tap in his hand.

The dripping had been keeping him awake at night and he had decided to try and sort it out without calling in a plumber.

A handyman Shaun Donnelly was not, as evidenced by the deluge of water that was gushing into the kitchen sink in his flat and the tap head he was holding, having twisted it until it had snapped off.

Technically it was up to his landlord to sort it out. The problem was that the flat owner lived in Manchester and it would probably take at least a day, if not two, to find someone who knew what they were doing.

He decided to consult his cousin despite knowing that the chances of him being of any help were slim to none. A bit like himself, Johnny was as useful as a chocolate hammer when it came to such matters.

As had become the norm, Johnny wasn't answering his phone.

A walk to the bar in the hope that someone might come to his rescue was the only other option.

In a foul mood he pulled on his coat and prepared to head out. As he was stomping down the front steps Magnus called to him.

'Well Shaun, how are things today?'

'Not great Magnus if I'm to be honest. I have to go here, I'm in a bit of a hurry.'

'Wait, what's wrong? Perhaps I can help.'

Unlikely, thought Loaf with a frown. But rather than be rude, he stopped to explain his predicament.

'I know just the boy,' replied Magnus, causing his friend's eyebrows to leap upward in surprise.

'You do? Who?'

'Archie. He's the caretaker here in the home. Come around and we'll walk over to his shed. He's a good old sort, if he can help you, he will.'

Twenty minutes later and Archie Faragher's legs were sticking out from under the sink of number 12 Westfield Terrace.

Magnus was grinning like a dog with a bone as they watched him work.

'See, I told you I knew a man,' he said proudly.

'I owe you one for this Magnus, I really do,' replied Loaf.

Archie reappeared, having replaced the broken tap and made sure it was properly plumbed in.

Taking off his battered baseball cap and scratching his greasy mop of hair, he announced that it should be at least 20 years before it needed fixed again.

'That's if it's treated properly and not twisted until it breaks of course,' he added with a barb that was obviously directed at Loaf.

'I'll be more careful the next time, I promise. Now, how much do I owe you Archie?'

'Don't worry about it, I owe Magnus a few quid from playing cards the other week. I'd say we're even after this, what do you reckon old timer?'

'You're a chancer Archie Faragher but okay,' Magnus answered with a smile.

Archie packed up his toolbox and said his goodbyes.

With the taps working again, Loaf was able to boil the kettle.

'Thank you for your help today Magnus, I don't know what I would have done without you.'

'Archie did all the work. But yes, no problem at all. How have been anyway Shaun, I haven't been chatting to you in a few days.'

Sitting himself down, Loaf explained about his plans to go back home for a couple of days.

Half-jokingly, he added, 'You'd hardly fancy going with me, would you?'

Magnus looked at him, shocked.

'Me? Visit Northern Ireland? I don't think so Shaun. I'm 85 for crying out loud. Thank you but my travelling days are done I'm afraid.'

The conversation moved on, Magnus telling him about an incident at dinner a few nights previous when one of the residents decided they were on a cruise.

'Mrs Archibald it was. She was convinced we were all at sea and that she could see the coast of America out the window. That birdbath in the garden, the one with the cherub, it was the Statue of Liberty apparently. To get her to settle down the nurses had to tell her we had reached shore and that it was time to get off. She was absolutely thrilled with it all, the poor old dear.'

Loaf laughed at the thought of it. In one sense it was sad, in the same way Mrs Hampton's situation was sad – a once healthy, articulate lady reduced to hallucinations and imaginary trips to the USA. But at the same time she was happy and she was safe with people around her to take care of her.

The more time he spent with Magnus, the more his attitude towards nursing home life was changing. Maybe it wasn't so awful after all.

'I've never been up here,' Magnus said, looking around the flat. 'It's quite nice, isn't it? Having your own space, your own little fortress where you can lock all the madness out, it's important Shaun. And if you're lucky one day you'll find a young lady like my Josie, someone to share your fortress with.'

'How do you know that I don't already have a young lady?'

'The dirty dishes over there by the sink. Those muddy slippers over there. The ring of grease on the cooker. If there was a woman about this place, she'd have you cleaning all that up and no arguments. Plus I would have seen her by now. I may be old but there's nothing wrong with my eyesight,' he winked as he put the cup of tea to his lips.

The cheeky wink made Loaf smile. Magnus Quayle was some character.

'Magnus, about coming to Ireland with me for a few days. Tell me you'll think about it at least. I'll set it all up, flight tickets, accommodation, the whole lot.'

'Thank you Shaun, but I doubt it,' came the snap reply.

'It'll be a chance to see Derry again. I'll book us a hotel. You can show me where The Irishman was and where you and Josie lived on Strand Road. I'd love to hear all about it.'

Magnus sighed as if he was being corralled into something he didn't want to do.

'Please Shaun, stop. I don't want to and let that be the end of it.'

Standing up and placing his mug on the sideboard, he added, 'I have to go, you look after yourself and if I'm not speaking to you before you leave, tell everyone back home I said hello.'

Without waiting for a reply, Magnus walked out the door.

Loaf watched from the window as he made his way back into Sunny View. He was still talking to himself and shaking his head when he disappeared out of sight.

Chapter Nineteen

Clubs were supposed to be fun.

Youth clubs, nightclubs, strip clubs, football clubs, even Fight Club looked like it might be entertaining if you weren't the one getting your face rearranged.

A death club on the other hand, it did not sound in the least bit enjoyable.

But it was what Abbey wanted to talk about.

Today's conversation was by far the longest and most serious since they had accidentally cyber-bumped into each other.

She started at the beginning, detailing how she had found the lump while on holiday with her friends. Over the next two hours she took him through the exhausting inventory of tests, probes, biopsies, medication, treatments and surgeries that had become her life.

Loaf marvelled continuously at the matter-of-fact way in which she was able to communicate her cancer journey and answer his questions.

Death clubs were a fairly recent phenomenon in Canada, Abbey explained, the aim being to provide a space where people could drink coffee and talk about dying.

'There was a time when I was really sick, I mean barely able to walk. I couldn't leave the house for seven months and I really struggled to keep my head straight.

'It was then that I realised I wanted to be able to talk about my own death. I didn't want to be afraid and I didn't want everyone else to be afraid.'

The first death club she went to was in nearby Whitney Springs. But it was poorly attended and a little too sombre for her liking.

'I got to thinking about how they were doing things and what I would like to see at such an event. I had to find a way to bring people in, to get them away from this notion that a death club is morbid and weird, something to be avoided. Because the bottom line here is that we're all going to have to face it one day, some of us sooner than others. But one day, somewhere down the road, it is going to be unavoidable.'

Her disappointing outing to Whitney Springs prompted her to establish Saint John's first death club. It was a much more casual, magazine-style affair, a galaxy away from the black shawls, rosary beads and long windy readings from the Bible.

Despite its host's enthusiasm, the club's first meeting had just five people at it.

'I know this might sound a bit cruel but I sort of forced my parents and my brothers to sit down and talk about death. It wasn't very nice but it was necessary because it is such a taboo subject.'

From a slow start, the monthly gatherings now attracted upwards of 30 people from the local area and from surrounding towns and villages.

'We talk about everything and it makes for a healthier, happier community,' she said. 'For example at our most recent session we had a palliative care doctor who explained what it's like when someone is dying.

'One of the best takeaways from that was, you know that rattle where at the very end you feel someone is gasping for breath? I saw it with my great-aunt and it frightened the life out of me. Well the palliative care doctor explained that when it gets to that stage, the person isn't gasping for breath, by that point they are too far gone and it's just bodily functions. That really settled my mind. That idea of someone suffering, when you can hear their last breath, is awful. But there's a comfort in knowing that they aren't in pain, do you not think?'

The heavy narrative was causing Loaf's shoulders to sag in the chair. And he could feel a headache coming on.

Not for the first time, she answered as if she had read his mind.

'I know this is heavy going and it's probably giving you a busting headache. But I want to get it all out there.

'I'll leave it at this and then I won't mention it again: Talking about death is important. By talking about your own death, you are taking control. You can have the funeral you want with the music you want. You can decide what the inscription is going to be on your headstone, rather than your family having to stress about whether they are doing the right thing or not.'

Loaf had never given one second's thought to what might be written on his headstone when he was gone. Who was going to get him a headstone? It would probably be one of his sisters unless he got busy in the children-making department fairly soon.

Maybe it was something he should start considering.

There was still one question he wanted to ask – 'How long do you have left to live?'

He even had it typed out and ready to send. At the very last second he deleted it though, too afraid of what the answer might be.

He wrote instead 'It has been a real laugh fest today, hasn't it:).'

'Ha! Welcome to my world Shaunie boy:)'

'I'll speak to you next week Abbey Vincent, same time, same place.x'

MAGNUS Quayle was laying on top of his bed, staring at the black and white photo of him and Josie on their wedding day.

They were outside St Eugene's Cathedral in Derry with the congregation throwing confetti over them.

Josie looked radiant in her long white dress, her veil pushed back from her smiling face. He didn't look too bad himself in his smartly tailored suit.

I miss you very much Josie Gillespie, he thought as he rested in the early afternoon silence.

He was still a little embarrassed at his exit from Shaun's flat. He had acted like a petulant child, storming off like that.

The truth was of course that he wasn't sure he could face it. He had never been in Derry without her. He would see her everywhere – posing by the cannons that lined the city's walls, twirling on the steps outside St Columb's Hall, sipping a Coca Cola on a bench by the River Foyle.

He knew too though that if she could somehow speak to him she would tell him to wise up, to get off his backside and pack his suitcase. Go and relive all the happy times they had spent together.

Back to Derry. After all these years.

He would have to apologise to Shaun and hope that the offer was still on the table.

Now was as good a time as any to go and knock on his door.

Magnus rang the bell three or four times without success. It was no great surprise, Shaun was a busy lad who always seemed to be going somewhere.

He was happy to wait. He wandered back to his chalet, made a cup of coffee and took up position at the hedge.

It was quiet today, not a single soul that he could chat to or wind up with his antics.

He was on his fourth cigarillo when Johnny's van pulled into the street.

Loaf got out and made straight for his flat, casting only a fleeting wave in Magnus's direction.

'A word Shaun, if I may please.'

'I'm pretty tired Magnus. What is it today,' he replied with a tinge of exasperation in his voice.

'It's about your trip home. Would there still be room for a handsome octogenarian do you think?'

Loaf's ears perked up. This was unexpected.

'There would, yes. Can I ask what has brought about this change of heart?'

'I had a quiet chat with a girl from Derry, the most beautiful creature the city has ever produced. She said I should go.'

'And right she is. I'll get the flights booked and I'll arrange accommodation. We leave on November 1, okay?'

'I'll check my busy schedule but that should be fine,' said Magnus.

Reaching into his breast pocket, he produced a bundle of £20 notes.

'This is to cover my share, I won't have you paying for everything. If it's not enough, come back to me, I have plenty more.'

Loaf gratefully accepted the money. Flights and hotels weren't cheap.

'I'm sure that's plenty Magnus,' he said, placing the money in his wallet. 'I'm going to need some details from you so I'll call over in the next day or two.'

'Should I apply for a passport? It's terribly short notice but I might be able to get an emergency one or something.'

'It's only a short internal flight, if you have any ID at all, it should be fine.'

'That's good. I'll see you soon Shaun. Derry here we come, eh,' he shouted excitedly.

TERRY was just finishing his first pint when Loaf walked in.

He had put in six late shifts in a row behind the bar and would have preferred to be spending his Monday evening on the sofa. But he had promised the Londoner they would meet up as soon as he got a night to himself.

With both of them settled and beers in front of them, Terry explained that his surname was Campbell, his father from Jamaica and his mother from Peckham.

He was a steel fixer by trade, a physically demanding job that entailed installing and tying together metal bars and mesh to strengthen concrete.

'All weathers, I'm out there,' he said, turning over a pair of palms so calloused they looked fireproof.

After a couple of drinks they decided to give Cheeko's Snooker and Pool Hall a go.

It was cold out and the chill ensured they added an inch to every step as they walked.

Cheeko's was busy and they had to wait 15 minutes to get a table.

Just as Loaf was about to break the balls Terry did something that both shocked and annoyed him.

Producing a little bag of white powder from the breast pocket of his shirt, he asked, 'Do you want a toot? It'll keep you dancing all night.'

'I do not, no. I've no time for that stuff at all.'

'Are you sure you're Johnny's cousin,' Terry laughed. 'Give me two seconds and I'll be back,' he shouted as he disappeared to the loo.

Johnny wasn't just drinking on their nights out then. Of course he had started snorting. He wouldn't have had the sense to say no. It explained why he had been so testy and paranoid of late.

As the night began to blur out of focus, so too did Loaf's judgement.

He had been determined to say nothing about the Harrison job. But with every sip his tongue loosened just a little bit more.

'Has Johnny mentioned anything to you about a wee mission we have coming up?'

'I don't think so, no. What sort of mission?'

'Have you ever come across a guy named Charlie Harrison?'

Unnecessarily loud dance music gave them little cause for concern that anyone might overhear.

'Charlie Harrison? I have actually. I was playing blackjack in the casino one night when he came around handing out free chips to every customer. It was his birthday or some such thing. When he looked at me with those villainous eyes, I knew right away that everything I'd heard about him was true.'

From Cheeko's they walked the short distance to The Green Parrot Pub just off Strand Street.

Loaf was really feeling the pace now and would gladly have sloped off home. But there was no sign of his drinking partner throwing in the towel. Quite the opposite in fact.

Pulling £20 from his wallet, Terry suggested they get a couple of shots to go with their beers.

'It's not my money so I don't give a fuck,' he laughed.

Taking up seats in the corner, Terry pressed him for more information about the upcoming job.

Loaf drunkenly obliged, divulging detail after detail.

'All the time you and Johnny have been spending together and he hasn't mentioned any of this? I find that hard to believe because he has big mouth on him. Anyway, me and him have talked and talked about it. The way we see it, our only option is to go through with it and hope that Harrison keeps his word. Once we deliver the shipment, he'll cut us loose and let us get on with our lives and our business.'

'Man, that's bad,' said Terry with a shocked look on his face. 'You come here to make an honest pound and a prick like that turns up giving it the big 'I am', taking advantage of ordinary salt of the earth folk like me and you. When is all this due to go down?'

'Early hours of December 2. Johnny is going to drive his van up, we're going to load it with gear at Castletown, make the drop in Ramsey and get the hell out of there.'

'But you're going to keep some of it for yourself, right?'

'What? No, no way. It's a straightforward transaction, moving it from one place to another. Besides, what would I do with a load of cocaine?'

'You might know a man who could make good use of it,' he said, patting the little baggie in his breast pocket. 'I could sell it and we could split the profits. Easy cash.'

'I'm sorry Terry but it's a very loud no from me. I just want this rubbish out of my road so I can get on with living my quiet life.'

'I understand. Well good luck with it brother, I hope it all goes according to plan.'

Two hours later and the party was still going. By now they were in The Underground, a nightclub where there were more staff than punters.

Loaf was so pissed he started wondering whether the banging was coming through the speakers or was inside his head.

Despite his drunken state, a comment Terry had made earlier in the evening continued to weigh on him.

'When I was going to buy beers earlier you said it wasn't your money. What did you mean,' he asked when the opportunity presented itself.

'The bed and breakfast I live in, it's run by some old dear who has dementia. She's constantly leaving money on the mantlepiece for the gas man or the window cleaner or the insurance guy. When she's not looking I help myself to it. The silly old goat never remembers if she left it out or not and just replaces it.'

'That's a terrible thing to do,' said Loaf, his blood getting up at the thought of it.

'Why? She's living in a ten-bedroom house and collecting rent from each of her lodgers. She must be minted. A couple of missing twenties will do her no harm.'

'I need to go home,' Loaf garbled to his drinking partner who was downing another Sambuca.

'No problem, I'll see you when I see you. Stay cool and don't be stressing. It'll all work itself out.'

Loaf staggered into the night air, glad to be out of Terry's company.

A Siberian wind was knifing through Douglas now and it helped him regain at least some of his faculties.

Two Tellies had been right, Terry was a wrong 'un.

How many times had he heard his mother say it? Every time he did something stupid in the throes of an alcoholic stupor – and there had been plenty of those over the years - she would be waiting for him the next morning with a smug smile on her face.

'Shaun Donnelly, when the drink is in, the wit is out.'

It was going to be a cold trek back to Westfield Terrace.

Plenty of time to wish he had kept his big mouth shut and said nothing.

Chapter Twenty

'Will you stay in place ya bony bastard.'

Johnny was trying to hang up a plastic skeleton which was showing zero desire to be impaled naked on a nail for all the world to see.

He eventually won the battle before stepping back to admire his handywork.

The bar looked well with its pumpkins, spider webs and other paraphernalia associated with the spookiest night of the year.

Loaf's mind was elsewhere though, namely on the following day's trip to Ireland.

It would have been so much simpler had he not invited Magnus. The pensioner had been at his door every day since they agreed they would travel together, asking question after question after question.

Are you sure you've the hotel booked? Does your mum not mind me dropping by? How are we getting to the airport? Seats, what about seats Shaun, have you booked extra legroom? I read once about this deep vein thrombosis you can develop when flying. Should I speak to my doctor about it?

It was exhausting. At the same time though it was nice to see the 85-year-old animated. By the sounds of it, he hadn't had much reason to get excited these past few years.

To be able to give him something to focus on, to look forward to, it did Loaf's soul good.

Their flight was at 11am, landing in Belfast at 11.35am. The chances of getting deep vein thrombosis on such a such a short plane journey were slim, he had assured his companion.

Before all that, there was the small matter of Halloween night which was either going to be mad busy or as dead as a zombie.

At 7pm it was starting to look like the latter with just two people sitting at the bar nursing pints. But ten minutes later a group of six young women walked in, all scantily dressed in the style of characters from Baywatch.

Loaf's first thought was that they must be freezing. Johnny was somewhat less considerate.

Eyeing a blonde in a skimpy bikini, he said, 'Would you look at that. At least I'll not have to worry about her being an undercover cop or reporter. Unless she's hiding a camera up her bajingo.'

The night only got busier from there with everyone from Dolly Parton to Michael Jackson to Mr Blobby making an appearance.

At 1am, with the party winding down but another two hours of cleaning still to be done, Loaf told his colleagues he would see them in a week or so.

As he was heading up the street Johnny called him back.

From his wallet he pulled a £20 note.

'Have a beer in The Barking Dog on me.'

It was a typically clumsy attempt to thaw the ice that had begun to separate them.

'Thanks Johnny but there won't be much drinking done. Keep your money and I'll see you in a few days.'

They lingered long enough for Loaf to look his cousin in the eye and wonder if he already knew he had revealed all to Terry.

Johnny looked back and wondered if Loaf already knew about the cocaine habit he was rapidly developing.

'Fair enough Shaun. But remember what I told you, not a word to anyone back home.'

'You giving me orders now Johnny, is that how it is?'

'Don't be like that. I'm just saying, for both our sakes.'

'I'll see you in a few days Johnny. And behave yourself.'

THE taxi to take them to the airport pulled into Westfield Terrace at 9am.

Magnus had been up since 6am, checking and rechecking to make sure he had packed for every eventuality. His less organised travelling partner was shoving clean underwear into his case at 8.45am, having only risen from his bed half an hour earlier.

At Ronaldsway Airport Loaf ordered a full English breakfast with a cup of tea and then complained the entire time he was eating it about the cashier charging him £14.99.

Magnus just kept looking around him, as if it was his first day on a new planet.

Not only had he never been on a plane, he had never been in an airport. Everything was an adventure – the check-in desk, the escalator, the planes stationary on the runway.

Onboard the aircraft Loaf swapped seats with him so the pensioner could see out the window. He also helped him master the seatbelt buckle when he couldn't work it out, but with the warning that the same service would not be extended should he need to use the loo.

By the time they reached altitude they were coming down again. Magnus watched in silent awe as they descended through the clouds into a grey looking Belfast City Airport.

After picking up their bags, a cab driver agreed to take them to the bus station where they would begin their journey by road to Ballyrush.

Magnus was considerably calmer as the bus pulled in, his fretting over the flight now behind him.

He dozed briefly as they journeyed over the Glenshane Pass before the bus turned left for Ballyrush.

It was nearing 3pm when they stepped down.

There to greet them, as she said she would be, was Martha.

Loaf had told her about Magnus over the phone, filling her in on his years spent living in Derry, how he had met Josie and their running The Irishman Pub on William Street together.

While he couldn't see her, his mum was smiling as he revealed his plans to bring his new friend over. It was just the sort of kind and thoughtful thing she would have expected of him.

Like when his father had taken him fishing. He couldn't have been more than six or seven at the time. On returning home Eddie said he had expected the boy to celebrate when he reeled in a small trout. Instead Loaf had burst into tears and told the dying fish it was going to be alright.

Martha Donnelly had plenty of reasons to be proud of the man her son had become.

After giving her a hug, Loaf introduced his mother to Magnus.

'Mrs Donnelly, you look young enough to be his sister.'

'That's very nice of you to say Mr Quayle. I only wish it were true.'

Hungry and weary, Loaf rolled his eyes at the little exchange.

'Can we go? And enough of this 'Mr Quayle' and 'Mrs Donnelly' rubbish. It's not Wuthering Heights you know.'

The arrangement was that they would spend two nights in Ballyrush before moving to the Maldron Hotel in Derry.

Despite her best efforts, Martha had not managed to rescue her daughter Catherine from the clutches of her lowlife partner.

Dana and Michael stayed over regularly but as of yet, Catherine had not found the strength to break free.

'Shaun, your room is where you left it and Magnus, I've made up the spare room for you,' she told them.

Following dinner, Magnus announced that he was going to turn in early.

'When you're used to spending your days doing very little, things like taxi, aeroplane and bus journeys tend to take it out of you. Good night Martha and thank you for your wonderful hospitality.'

In his absence, Loaf and his mother talked for hours. She filled him on what his two sisters were up to as well as the local goings-on. She already knew all about The Thirsty Sailor – only the good stuff mind you - and was surprised that her wayward nephew appeared to be making a go of it.

'I was sure he'd be up to his neck in trouble by now, smuggling drugs or some such badness. He had his mother's heart broke you know…'

As she relayed again all the teary phone calls from Johnny's mother, Loaf thought to himself mum, if only you knew.

He eventually got around to telling her about Abbey Vincent and her illness.

'Do you love this girl?

'I've never met her.'

'That's not what I asked you.'

'I don't know mum. I like her a lot. But this whole terminal cancer thing, what am I supposed to do?'

'Son, apart from to yourself, you haven't a single responsibility in this world. No wife, no children, no mortgage, you can go anywhere in the world and do anything you want. Why don't you take some time off and go and visit her, find out more about her. If it doesn't work out romantically, you'll still have a friend. And hey, who knows, maybe it is meant to be. Maybe she is the one. The Lord moves in mysterious ways you know.'

He had always fancied visiting Canada. It struck him as being like America but without the obesity and unedifying hubris.

His mum's wise counsel was exactly what he needed to hear.

THEIR time in Ballyrush passed quickly, spent showing Magnus the few sights worth seeing and catching up with the few friends worth catching up with.

Martha was sorry to see them leave but was pleased to hear that her boy planned to ring in the New Year with her.

'I'll work up until December 29 and then I'll catch a flight home. I'll see you soon mum,' he said as they prepared to leave.

As Loaf had assured her he would be, Magnus proved to be every bit the gentleman.

'Maybe you'll come to the Isle of Man. Coffee with milk and two sugars, am I right?'

'That's correct Magnus. And yes, I will have to get over and see this bar that is taking up all of my son's time. He's thinner than the last time I saw him, I just hope he's looking after himself.'

'I'll keep an eye on him Martha, you don't have to worry on that front. You take care and thank you again.'

THE number 98 bus took them towards Derry, Magnus marvelling at the various villages they passed through on their way to the city.

As they approached the Craigavon Bridge his eyes widened at the sight before him.

The last time he had seen the quay along the cityside of the River Foyle it had been an industrial conveyor belt of maritime, grain, coal and livestock companies.

That was all gone, replaced by a bright, modern and welcoming European-style waterfront.

Driving down John Street, he stared up at Foyleside, a high-reaching shopping mall with adjoining multi-storey car park.

They got off at Foyle Street and Loaf suggested they go for a pint before checking in.

But the idea was quickly over-ruled.

'Let's go and drop off our bags first. Then we'll get a pint. I haven't had a drink in years but I think I'm going to need one.'

After picking up their key cards and quickly surveying their respective rooms, they started out.

Magnus insisted that they walk along the docks first.

'It's busier than Douglas prom,' he remarked as Loaf wondered if he was ever going to see that pint.

'Stop being so impatient,' Magnus frowned, seeing the look on the face beside him. 'None of this is new to you but it is to me. When I left this city it was in the grip of The Troubles. Do you know how many people were killed in Northern Ireland the year we got out? It was close to 500. Some of them were friends of ours, men who would come in for a drink and a chat.'

The sun's rays were glistening off the Foyle's surface. On the opposite bank a train's horn sounded as it set off on its journey to Belfast.

Gripping the railings, Magnus watched it until it turned the corner and disappeared out of sight.

'It was a different world back then,' he said quietly.

Their first drink was in Hardy's on Waterloo Street. The young barmaid placed two lovely looking pints of stout on the counter.

From his pocket Magnus produced a disposable camera and asked her if she wouldn't mind taking a photograph of them.

She happily obliged, encouraging them to hold up their glasses and smile.

Magnus took a hefty slug of Guinness and tried to remember the last time he had held a pint in his hand.

Done, they decided it was time to take the short walk on to William Street.

What they would find there was anyone's guess.

Chapter Twenty one

Rounding the corner, Magnus was pleased to see that The Irishman, while no longer called that, was still a pub.

His fear was that it might have been pulled down or turned into something else, like one of those awful money lending shops that seemed to be popping up everywhere.

Loaf pushed the door to The Free Derry Arms. It was deserted apart from the barman and a single customer sat in the corner reading his newspaper.

Magnus stood in the middle of the floor, trying mentally to put everything back in its place.

Above the fireplace there used to be a clock with a pendulum hanging down. Where it once was there was now a widescreen television.

In The Irishman of old there were shelves that ran above head height around the bar. On them sat brass pots and urns that were the decoration of choice at the time.

The shelves were gone and no wonder, thought Magnus. They had been an awful pain to dust and keep clean.

'And over in that corner there was a piano that came to life on the odd occasion someone with the ability to play it dropped in and gave us a song,' he explained to Loaf.

The piano was no more, in its place two gambling machines.

The walk down memory lane was shattered by the bartender.

'Can I get you gentlemen something or did you just come in for the heat,' he asked with a smile.

'Sorry pal,' replied Loaf acknowledging the pleasant nudge to buy a drink. 'Yes, we'll have two Guinness please.'

As he was pouring the story was told, Magnus explaining all about how he had first set eyes on his future wife standing where the barman was right now.

'So you used to own this place back in the 1960s,' asked the inquisitive gentleman in the corner, folding his paper and putting it away.

'Josie and I did, yes, we took it over from her father, Myles Gillespie. Myles and his wife Biddie and their two daughters, Josie and Winnie, lived upstairs, as did I briefly.'

'I'm Charlie Curry, the current owner,' he introduced himself. 'It's lovely to meet you…'

'Magnus. Magnus Quayle.'

'It's lovely to meet you Magnus. Look, let me get you lads that pint and if you're happy to, we can sit and have a chat. I'm from just up the road and I'd love to hear more about your time here.'

For the next two hours Magnus happily rolled back the years to when men wore ties and jackets to the pub and when Guinness came in bottles rather than keg.

Paddy Sharkey, Jackie Gorman, Teddy O'Brien, Ruby Patton – he remembered them all clearly despite the passing of so many years.

One of the customers Magnus recalled was Sylvester English, a huge guy with a beard who could drink pints like they were water.

'Sylvester was my great-uncle,' revealed Charlie Curry with delight. 'An absolute horse of a man. He only died last year you know.'

Charlie waited until they had finished their pints before asking them if they would like to see upstairs.

'There's nothing up there now, it's just storage space. This place has changed hands that many times over the years so God only knows when the flat you lived in was pulled apart.'

The entrance was the same, out the back door and up a narrow flight of stairs. But inside, Charlie was right, there was nothing left that resembled accommodation.

Magnus explained the layout – the little kitchen, the living area and the two bedrooms, one of which he and Josie had shared with Winnie.

'Can you imagine it, me, Josie and Winnie sleeping in one room and then Myles and Biddie in the other, five of us living up here. It didn't seem this small at the time.'

As he wandered around the place where their bedroom used to be, his eyes were drawn to the windowsill.

They were faint after years of being painted over. But they were there, two letters carved into the wood.

'JG - Josie Gillespie,' he gasped, running his fingers over the grooves. 'She must have carved it when she was a young girl.'

Charlie and Loaf gathered round to see the engraving.

'That's fantastic,' said Charlie warmly, placing his hand on Magnus's shoulder. 'Wait here a second,' he ordered as an idea came to him.

After dashing downstairs, he returned with a small screwdriver which he offered to Magnus.

'Go on.'

'Go on what?'

'Put your initials beside Josie's.'

'Can I? You don't mind me damaging your windowsill?'

'Your love story is a bit more important, wouldn't you agree?'

Magnus got to work, scoring MQ below the JG that had been engraved many decades earlier.

'There you are,' said Charlie, once he was done. 'JG and MQ, together forever. The way it was meant to be.'

Magnus's eyes filled up as he traced his fingers over the lettering.

'Together forever. Thank you Mr Curry, this means a lot.'

'No problem Magnus. You have given me quite a tale to tell.'

ST EUGENE'S Cathedral had barely changed in the years since Magnus and Josie had walked down the aisle.

They both lit candles, Loaf first sending a private blessing all the way across the Atlantic to Canada and then one back to Ballyrush and to his mum.

From there they made their way to the nearby cemetery, the plan being to say a prayer at the graveside of Myles and Biddie Gillespie. But among the thousands of burial plots, they were unable to find the headstone they were looking for.

'It's been so long,' Magnus sighed sadly. 'But our intentions were good and I'm sure that counts for something.'

The afternoon was pressing on. Loaf suggested that they walk down Strand Road to where Magnus had once lived. To his surprise the older man said he would prefer to go back to the hotel.

'I'm just feeling a bit a tired, that's all Shaun. Between the walk up that hill to the cemetery and those couple of pints yesterday, I'm done in. I'll be as right as rain after a nap. Come and knock on my door at 6pm and we'll go for dinner.'

Loaf used his free time to revisit some of the bars he used to frequent. A game of darts there, a frame of pool here, it was the perfect way to knock out an afternoon.

That evening over burgers and chips the two of them chatted about their adventure so far.

'It has been lovely,' said Magnus. 'Seeing your home place, meeting your mum, getting back to the bar and meeting Mr Curry, I never thought for a second I would be in Derry again.'

'That's good to hear Magnus, I'm very glad you're enjoying yourself. I am too, it's exactly what I needed before I go back to work. We've a thing coming up that I'm not looking forward to. But there's no way out of it.'

Naturally the vague remark sparked Magnus's curiosity. And while Loaf had spent weeks wishing he hadn't blabbed all to Terry, he had no problem telling Magnus. In fact it felt only right that a Manx man should know about the nefarious activities taking place on his island.

He wasn't as shocked at the news as Loaf thought he might be.

'Charlie Harrison? I can't say I know him. But it doesn't surprise me. Going back to when I had The Hook, Line and Sinker, there were guys trying it on then too. But the business community was tight back then, everyone knew everyone and by standing together we were able to face them down. I doubt if there is still that community spirit today. I hope you're going to report the matter to the police.'

'It's not that simple Magnus unfortunately. But it'll be fine. Another few weeks and we'll be out from under him.'

'You can't be serious, you're going to go through with it? Come on Shaun, you're too smart to be that stupid. You do realise you'll end up doing ten years if you're caught? It's not a game son, this is for real. Ten years of your life, locked away in a tiny prison cell. Do yourself a favour and stay well away from it all.'

Loaf took a bite from his burger and stared out across Waterloo Place. Literally and figuratively he chewed, trying to digest what Magnus had just advised him.

As he did so his phone began to ring.

It was Johnny. He had asked his cousin not to contact him unless it was something serious.

It would have been bad manners to get up and step outside to take a call mid-meal so he let it go to voicemail.

Ten minutes later he excused himself and walked to the bathroom.

'Shaun, there's been a development and not a good one for us. Harrison rang me last night. Phone me back and I'll fill you in.'

He pressed the call button and waited.

'What's up Johnny?'

'You know that thing we have to do? Well the on-shore team that Harrison spoke to us about has fallen through. It's just me and you and we're going to need our life jackets. I'll say no more until I see you but that's the situation.'

Loaf shook his head in frustration. He wasn't fond of half-stories.

'Right, I'll be home tomorrow night. I'll speak to you then.'

This was getting absurd. He rinsed his face in cold water and looked at himself in the mirror.

'You're too smart to be this stupid Shaun,' he told his reflection.

MAGNUS sat himself down on the steps of the Guildhall.

It was just after 6am on their last day, too early to be disturbing his friend.

A red dawn was battling its way successfully through the morning clouds.

He was alone, bar the pigeons that were pecking around the square in front of him.

He had the whole city to himself, or at least that was how it felt.

Watching as the birds swooped up and flew off, he began to take stock.

While for the most part he was glad he had made the trip, there was just a little corner of himself that was tinged with sadness.

The visit had brought him closer to Josie but it had also made her seem further away than ever.

One more dance, one more night at the cinema, one more ice cream hand in hand along Chamberlain Street. He would have given everything to have just one of those days again.

He had realised many years ago that the saying 'time is a healer' was a falsehood. The longing and the loneliness never healed, you just learned to live with them.

Back at the hotel, Loaf was up and dressed. They still had one more visit to make before catching their flight back.

He could sense the reluctance in Magnus's step as they neared number 47 Strand Road.

Loaf wondered if the trip had become a bit much for the pensioner, a sort of memory overload that he was struggling to process.

The property was still an abode and a well maintained one at that.

Two large flowerpots flanked the white PVC front door while in the window sat a vase of fresh flowers.

'I'll knock if you don't want to,' offered Loaf. 'I can explain why we're calling and knowing Derry people, we'll be invited in for a cuppa. Or we can give it a miss altogether. It's up to you.'

Magnus hardly heard him. In his mind he was watching his wife cleaning the windows, humming along to a song that was playing on the wireless. Next door he could see Mrs Butler sitting out on her favourite chair, her dog Finn on her knee.

He and Josie had loved it here.

Magnus, did you hear me?'

'You know what Shaun, I think we'll just leave it. This is someone else's home now, they don't need an old codger like me coming around and dragging up the past. If they are half as happy as I was then they'll be doing alright.'

Looking at his watch, Magnus added, 'We should start making a move, I don't know about you but I'm ready for home.'

IT was just after 8pm when their plane touched down on the tarmac at Ronaldsway Airport.

They were both exhausted and looking forward to climbing into their respective beds.

As they waited for a taxi Magnus lit up one of his cigarillos. Little was said between them as he smoked, such was the fatigue.

The cabbie chatted and chatted as he drove them to Douglas. Loaf nodded along in the front seat beside him, thankful it was a speech rather than a Q&A.

He could hear Magnus snoring lightly behind him, out for the count after a long day on the move.

After being dropped off they walked the length of Westfield Terrace together, the rumble of the wheels of their luggage the only sound against the evening silence.

'I'll sleep tonight,' Magnus yawned for the thousandth time as they prepared to part company.

'Me too. I'll see you tomorrow, okay? We'll get a coffee and do a full debrief then, how does that sound?'

'That sounds like a plan. Drinking pints at my age, who would have thought it eh?'

As he was about to walk away, Magnus called his name.

'Shaun.'

'Yes Magnus.'

There was a pause as if the older man was thinking about what to say.

'Thank you. Thank you for everything.'

Loaf smiled and nodded.

'I'll see you in the morning sir. Good night Magnus.'

He dragged himself up the steps of number 12, his only thought that in a few minutes he would be curled up under his duvet.

Behind him the rattle of a suitcase being pulled became fainter. He paid it little heed as he fumbled in his pockets for his keys.

Suddenly though the noise stopped. A loud groan followed by a clatter filled the air.

Loaf sprinted down the slight incline in the direction of the gates to Sunny View Care Home.

There he found a body laying crumpled face down in the road.

He turned his friend over and called his name, urging and pleading him back to life.

But there was nothing he could do.

Chapter Twenty Two

His heart had given up they said.

One of the nurses in Sunny View revealed that he had been living with coronary artery disease for years.

It was a condition common among the elderly, she explained.

The more Loaf thought about it, the more he wondered how he hadn't spotted there was something wrong with him.

That time when he fell over and broke his hip. The need to stop and take a break every ten minutes while they were walking.

But then again, how was he to know? As far as he was concerned these were just things related to his age and the regularity with which Magnus smoked his little brown cigarillos.

Loaf looked down at his friend, laid out in a suit and tie, his hair and moustache styled the way he always liked to wear it. He would have appreciated the effort put in to making him look smart. Sartorial elegance was important to him.

Martha Donnelly burst into tears when her son revealed the news to her.

'But he seemed so chirpy when he was here,' she wept down the phone while vowing to travel over as soon as she could get a flight.

In the moments after the collapse Loaf had dashed to the care home for help.

Consumed by a fog of panic he struggled to get the words out.

Standing now in the quiet of McAuley's Funeral Home he could remember little, other than a sudden rush to try and revive the pensioner followed by a blur of flashing blue lights and emergency service personnel asking what had happened.

'One minute he was fine and the next he was gone,' was all he could tell them.

Among those who came to pay their respects was Josie's sister Winnie. She was 91 and lived in Glasgow. After Josie's death she and Magnus had kept in touch by post. They hadn't spoken in a long time but did exchange Christmas cards every year without fail.

She had learnt of his passing through her son who had spotted his death notice on the internet.

Loaf filled her in on their Derry adventure, including the detail about the initials on the windowsill.

'Oh I remember it well,' she laughed daintily. 'I was just about to start carving my name as well when daddy caught us. He went ballistic, grounded us for a week and no pocket money for a month.

'Daddy had great time for Magnus you know. While he never said it, Josie and I knew he worried terribly that we would marry men who weren't good to us. When Magnus came along with his smart dress sense and courteous way, daddy was delighted.

'Now they're all gone, mummy, daddy, Josie, Magnus,' she said with a sad little sigh. 'The card list gets shorter every year.'

They were both called to a meeting where it was revealed that Magnus had not left a will. Questions were being asked about a next of kin.

Winnie was adamant that her name should not be put forward. At her age she hadn't the strength to be dealing with a matter of such importance.

'You seemed to be as close to him as anyone. I think you should deal with his estate. As much as I liked Magnus, I can't say that I really knew the man. Besides I can't be spending weeks and months here sorting through his personal belongings and waiting to sign legal documents.

'My only request would be that his remains are cremated and scattered in the same place as Josie. I do recall him expressing that wish all those years ago when we were stood on the pier at Peel.

'If we can agree on that Shaun then I'm happy to leave everything else with you.'

The funeral was held in Peel Cathedral. It was a lowkey affair, the congregation made up largely of staff from Sunny View and a handful of people who remembered Magnus from his days running The Hook, Line and Sinker.

Martha gripped her son's hand as the priest began to deliver his eulogy.

'Some of you here will remember Magnus Quayle from his years as a publican, first in The Irishman in Northern Ireland and later in The Hook, Line and Sinker here in Peel.

'I did not know Magnus personally but from what I have learnt of him over these past few days he was a kind gentleman, someone who would never see a customer stuck for a drink on days when the price of a pint could not be mustered.'

Raising a gentle ripple of laughter from the congregation, he quickly added, 'Before anyone reports me to the bishop, I am in no way condoning the consumption of alcohol. But I am sure the Lord would have approved of such generosity.

'I am told too that Magnus lived for his wife Josie. According to those who knew them, you rarely saw one without the other. Josie was his reason to get up out of bed every morning and the strength that carried him through each day.

'When Josie passed away Magnus left the hospitality business and moved into Sunny View Care Home. Such a change would have been tough for him. Yet despite his grief it would appear he did find his place in the world again among the staff and residents of Sunny View who will miss him dearly.

'Speaking to one of his carers just this morning, she described Magnus as a warm and amiable man but in many ways a private individual. Never shy when it came to having a chat but someone who had few close friends. That was until earlier this year when a new neighbour ignited a fresh spark in him.'

Ignited a fresh spark in him? Loaf glanced sideways at his mother. He could see she was stifling her laughter because she was thinking the same as him. That it sounded like he and Magnus were a couple.

He was briefly tempted to put his hand up, to interrupt and tell everyone that they were just mates. But he let it go as the priest continued with his commentary.

'Shaun Donnelly is present here today along with his mum Martha. And over the last few days I've had the opportunity to speak to this impressive young man. He explained how he and the deceased became pals quite by accident.

'As luck, or the Lord, would have it, Shaun was born just up the road from the city of Derry where Magnus's late wife Josie was from.

'Shaun is also a barman so as you can imagine, he and Magnus had plenty to talk about.

'A few weeks ago, while planning a visit back home to Northern Ireland, Shaun decided to invite Magnus to join him. A young man befriending an elderly pensioner, I'm sure you'll agree that such gestures are rare in today's society.

'They spent a number of days in Derry, days which I have no doubt meant the world to Magnus.

'Sadly their trip ended on the note that brings us all together here today. But thanks to you Shaun, Magnus Quayle left this world with many lovely memories and with joy in his heart.'

Starting to sound a bit gay there again padre thought Loaf, mentally encouraging the clergyman to wrap it up.

'If we can all bow our heads now and pray that Jesus and all the angels and saints will open the gates of heaven and invite our brother Magnus in, where no doubt his beloved Josie will be waiting for him.'

Following the service there was lots of handshaking, everyone keen to meet the man who had apparently reignited Magnus's spark.

From the church, Magnus's remains were transported to the local crematorium.

There, final prayers were said before a classical version of How Great Thou Art began to play.

Loaf put his arm around his mum's shoulder and pulled her in close as the coffin carrying his friend disappeared from view.

ABBEY Vincent expressed great sadness when told of Magnus's death.

'At least you were there with him. He died with his best friend at his side. It's not a bad way to go really. And Shaun he was 85 and had lived a long and eventful life by the sounds of it. Obviously I never met the man but I don't think he would have had too many complaints.'

It was true, 85 was an age few lived to see. And to go like that, quickly, quietly and without a fuss, it was what he would have wanted.

If there was one thing Abbey knew about it was mortality. She had been living with the worst kind of illness, one that was going to eventually kill her, for years.

Magnus's passing had prompted in Loaf deep questions about religion and what comes next. Was there a 'next'? Where was Magnus now? Was an angelic Josie really waiting with open arms to greet her husband following his departure from the earthly soil? Or was it all just a nonsense, a fairy story dreamt up to control the masses through the threat of God's swift and terrible wrath?

If he wanted an informed opinion on such theological matters then he need look no further than the woman from Saint John who was messaging him right now.

'Do you believe in God,' he asked.

'I do. I used to pray a lot when I was stuck in bed. My grandmother and I were really close and when I was lying there feeling sorry for myself, I would feel her presence in the room with me.

'I also have a lovely friendship with our local priest, Fr Neeson. He's not like a normal priest, he's much cooler. He comes around a couple of times in the month and sits with me. We talk about politics, we talk about whatever the environmental catastrophe of the day is, we just talk. He's a lovely man.

'On top of that my mother has half the world praying for me and I feel them. When I'm feeling low I get this warm glow that someone or something is looking after me.

'So to answer your question yes, I do believe in a higher power.'

The firmness of her opinion helped.

Loaf would miss his friend and all his little eccentricities. Since his arrival on the island Magnus had been a permanent feature in his life, standing daily at his hedge wishing him well as he headed off to work.

There would no more of those days. But Magnus would be around, Loaf could sense it.

Chapter Twenty Three

There was talk of a big freeze.

Temperatures had plummeted to minus two with forecasters suggesting the mercury could reach as low as minus seven in the coming days.

It was less than 48 hours until they were due to go and collect the drugs for Charlie Harrison.

Loaf had made up his mind. His decision was not going to be to his cousin's liking.

Not that it mattered anymore. They'd hardly spoken since his return from Derry. Johnny hadn't bothered coming to the funeral and during the one brief telephone conversation they'd had, Magnus's passing wasn't even mentioned.

All he'd said was that 'the mission' was no longer just transporting the packages in the back of the van. They also had to row out and bring them back to shore.

One of the men who was supposed to sail out and fetch them had fallen and broken his leg. His partner said there was no way he was working with anyone else.

From being as meek as a mouse that evening in Charlie Harrison's house, Johnny now appeared to be looking forward to their little trip.

Something had changed.

According to the other bar staff he was spiralling out of control.

Carl reported how one morning he had turned up for his shift to find the bar strewn with smashed glasses and empty baggies.

'It's got pretty messy, I think he's losing the plot,' said the barman.

LOAF had just locked the front door of The Thirsty Sailor when he heard a key being inserted from outside.

It was late and he was tired. The bad weather had made it a long and uneventful Thursday night.

A grunt of acknowledgement from his cousin told him all was not well.

Johnny walked straight across the freshly mopped floor and began pouring himself a pint.

Nothing was said until he sat himself down on a bar stool. From where he was stood Loaf could clearly see the trace of white powder below his left nostril.

His first question did little to ease the tension.

'Shaun did you tell anyone about this wee thing we have to do tomorrow night?'

From the moment he had blabbed everything to Terry, he knew that his drunken cockiness would come back to bite him.

He kept mopping for a few seconds before replying.

'I don't know what you're on about,' he fibbed.

Johnny smirked.

'That was a wee test Shaun. I've known for weeks that you told Terry.'

'Fair enough, I did mention it to him. I thought I could trust him. Clearly I was wrong.'

'If you told Terry, who else have you been talking to? How do I know you haven't told others? How do I know you haven't been slabbering it all over Douglas? Maybe you've alerted the police so they'll be waiting for us. Then you can pin all this on me and take over this place yourself. Is that your game Shaun?'

Loaf looked at him and the sorry sight he had become. He was overweight and unkempt, his skin was greasy and he had a nasty cold sore on his lip.

He needed help and on another day Loaf would have been happy to offer some cousinly assistance.

But it wasn't what Johnny had come looking for. He had seemingly convinced himself, in his twisted, paranoid mind, that his head barman was conspiring with the cops to take everything from him.

What he was conveniently overlooking of course was how they had arrived at this point in the first place.

'Tell me this Johnny, of the two of us which one was stupid enough to spill their guts to an undercover reporter? I'll give you a clue, it wasn't me. If you had been thinking with your wee small brain instead of with your wee small dick we wouldn't be in this mess. So don't be coming in here all drugged up throwing your weight around. You and Terry, the cocaine kings, out making a show of yourselves. You think I don't know you've been snorting that shit? Of course I know, look at the state of you.'

His voice was raised now, his temper roaring in his ears.

'I don't give a damn anyway because I'm out,' Loaf went on. 'You can go and pick up Harrison's drugs on your own. I'm having no part in it.'

If he was expecting Johnny to be shocked or wounded by the news then he was wrong.

'You know what Shaun? I don't give a flying fuck whether you come with me or not. You're a joke, that's what you are. You coming over here was supposed to be fun, me and you, beers and birds. But all you've done is mope about with a big serious head on you. You were heartbroken over that Abbey slag and her riding half of Douglas. And that old fossil who lived in the care home beside your flat. Any wonder he croaked, you probably depressed him to death.'

Johnny's eyes were wild in his head. He was like a man possessed with the cocaine coursing through his system.

Loaf leapt at him, catching him with a right hook that sent him to the floor.

It was a reactionary punch, delivered without forethought or malice. He was as shocked as his cousin. But as he advanced to offer an apology and a hand up, Johnny kicked out and swept the legs from under him.

He went to the ground with an almighty slap, cracking his head on the still wet tiles.

Johnny scrambled to his feet first. Towering over his stricken cousin who was desperately clambering on to all fours he came forward with a boot that caught him square in the ribs.

It was a low act, kicking a man when he was down. But he was out of control, like a car without brakes as he staggered backwards until he found the pool table. He lifted a cue and was just about to smash it over Loaf's head when a voice from somewhere pulled him back.

He put the stick down and slowly squatted down on his hunkers. Out of breath, he put his head in his hands.

'If you had just listened to me for another second before throwing punches, what I was going to say was that you actually did us a favour,' Johnny said, wiping spittle from his face.

'I was going to tell you that Terry and Andy are coming with us. See, after you got drunk and told Terry all about the operation he couldn't wait to pull Andy aside up on the building site. They talked about it and came to an agreement. Then they practically sprinted down here to have a private word with me.'

If Johnny thought bringing Terry on board was a clever move then he truly was a fool. Terry was a thief, a crook and a junkie who would stab him in the back as soon as look at him.

As for Andy, a drunk monkey riding a blind horse could see that he wasn't to be trusted.

And wasn't Andy supposed to be keeping a low profile after the Hannah Asher mess?

'Harrison said Andy can't be involved. I was there when he told us Johnny.'

'Charlie Harrison? That old bastard? Fuck Charlie Harrison. We've got it all sorted. You see Andy and Terry, they're a couple of smart lads. Andy has done this sort of job before. He knows people, people bigger than Charlie Harrison. Between the three of us we've concocted a plan, one that is going to make us a load of cash.

'Come on Shaun, come with us. This is it, our ticket to the big time. I'm sorry about all this tonight, I don't know what came over me. Say you'll do it Shaun, me and you, Butch and Sundance.'

They were both standing now, Loaf leaning on the bar counter holding his ribs. His eye was rapidly swelling from where he had thumped it off the floor.

He was a spent force. But the rage in him was like nothing he'd never felt before.

Johnny was walking away from him when he hooked him around the neck until he had him in a choke hold. He hauled him backwards so the two of them tumbled over on to the floor.

If kicking a man when he was down wasn't a particularly gallant act, neither was attacking a man from behind.

But if he let go now, one of them was going to end up dead.

As they wrestled and writhed, a bag fell from Johnny's pocket. He rolled over on to it, causing its contents to explode in a cloud of white powdery dust.

'FUUUUUUUCCCCKKKKK,' he roared. 'I'll kill you Shaun, I swear I'll fucking kill you.'

But Loaf had him. There was no escape. If he wanted, he could keep tightening his arm until his cousin was out cold.

'Have you had enough,' he asked while maintaining his iron hold, the back of his cousin's head almost touching his teeth.

'Garrrghhghhgh,' Johnny gargled, unable to get any more words out. With his face turning purple, he just about managed to nod to indicate that he was done.

Loaf loosened his grip and the two of them fell back, completely drained.

Prostrate, Johnny gulped down big mouthfuls of air and tried to readjust his sight.

'Jesus…' he bellowed, his chest pounding.

Unlike his cousin, Loaf still had his senses about him. And he was in no mood for forgiveness.

Back on his feet he shouted furiously, 'You know what you can do Johnny Donnelly? 'You can go fuck yourself. You're a loser, always were, always will be.

'Your own parents couldn't stand the sight of you, they literally paid to see the back of you.

'How many times did I protect you Johnny, answer me that? All those times at school when the others were poking fun at you, calling you fatty and Johnny Ten Bellies. Who stood up for you? The time Arsenal Doherty challenged you to a scrap out the back lane because he said you called his mum a slag? Who went out to bat for you then? I took a right hammering too.

'And now look at you. Over here acting the big dog, tied up with absolute scumbags.

'You, Terry and Andy can go right ahead and do whatever you want with Harrison's cocaine. In fact why don't the three of you grab it and chuff it up your noses like the wankers that you are?

'I'm out Johnny. I'm out of tomorrow night's job and I'm out of this place.

'Those two are going to betray you, I would stake my life on it. But you go right ahead.

'I hope for the sake of your mother and father you don't get caught. But if you do, don't be sending me prison visit invitations.'

A cough sent a jagged pain shooting through his body. He was broken but he couldn't look at his cousin for one more second.

He staggered out the door, leaving Johnny alone in a mess of blood and cocaine.

It was over. It was all over.

Chapter Twenty Four

It hadn't snowed in the Isle of Man for nine years.

Tonight it was as if the island was inside a glass globe and someone had given it an almighty shake.

Johnny drove cautiously along the promenade, relieved to see it deserted apart from a stray dog that was sniffing around one of the bins.

After parking in his usual spot, he ran from the van to the pub door.

The flakes tumbled heavily on to his coat as he stuck the key in the door and tried to get it to turn.

Inside he looked at his watch. It was 1.30am. They had agreed to meet at 1.45am, the rendezvous at Castletown scheduled for 2.30am.

Five minutes later his two partners in crime arrived. As agreed, they came in by the back door.

Andy sat them down and took them through what was going to happen. The captain aboard the mother ship would text him once the drop had been made. He and Terry would row out and collect the watertight bales. Johnny would remain on shore, keeping an eye for any sign of human life. In the unlikely event that a straggler or insomniac should make an appearance, he was to text Andy to let him know it was not safe to land.

Once they were safely docked, the drugs would be bundled into the van and taken to their final destination.

Terry suggested they have a pint before setting off. But the idea was shot down by both other parties who agreed that sharp minds would be required for the next few hours.

After Loaf had left Terry in The Underground nightclub, the big steel fixer had gone to the bar and asked for a pen and paper.

Before the details were wiped from his memory by the copious amount of drink and drugs he had consumed, he jotted down what he had been told:

Charlie Harrison

Cocaine shipment

Early hours December 2

Castletown pier to drop-off point in Ramsey

Two days later he had made a point of bumping into Andy and asked if he could have a chat. In no shape or form were they friends and had it been anything else other than a chance to make a fortune, Terry would have gone nowhere near the sneering Irish man.

His disdain for him stemmed from the fact that he was a stone cold racist. He didn't even try to hide it. One time in the building site canteen Terry had bought a banana for his lunch. On seeing it Andy had piped up in front of the rest of the lads, 'I thought they would feed you enough of those in the zoo'. In any other setting Terry would have ripped the head from his shoulders, something he could easily have done given their size difference. But such a reaction would have cost him his job which he could ill-afford to lose. So he let it slide. For now.

Andy was surprised at being approached by the Londoner and even more surprised when he laid out what he knew.

He knew that Andy worked for Charlie Harrison. He also knew quite a bit about what was due to go down on December 2.

Andy initially denied any knowledge of the operation and warned Terry he should mind his tongue if he wished to keep it.

By afternoon tea break though his tune had changed.

'What are you thinking big man?'

'I'm thinking that we team up, steal the shipment and sell it ourselves. Not the four of us, just you and me. We would make millions from it.'

'And how do you propose we do this?'

'Easy. We – me, you, Loaf and that idiot cousin of his - collect the gear in Castletown as planned. On the way to Ramsey we ambush them, kill them and dump their bodies in the sea. When we're asked what went down we say they did the dirty on us, that they pulled a gun and made us get out of the van. We tell Harrison the last two things we saw were the tail-lights as they drove off.

'He'll think that Johnny and Loaf ripped him off with the intention of smuggling the coke back to Ireland. All we have to do is hide the gear, keep quiet for a few months before shipping the load to England where I know a guy who will give us a decent price for it. Easy.'

'You've all this mapped out in that crazy African head of yours haven't you.'

'I'm half-Jamaican you ignorant pig,' countered Terry, adding the remark to Andy's account.

Terry Campbell had grown up in south London. He was nine when his father was killed in an industrial accident, leaving his mother to bring up five children on her own.

Despite her best efforts to keep him in school and out of trouble, the streets got him.

Shoplifting, pickpocketing and drug dealing all became daily components of his young life.

'Growing up, if I saw an opportunity to make a quid, I grasped it,' he told Andy. 'It's the same now and if that makes me a bastard, then so be it. This right here, this deal going down on

December 2, it's the biggest opportunity that has ever come my way.

'I'm not going to let it pass me by and neither should you.'

Andy liked it. He was becoming tired of being Charlie Harrison's lapdog. Eight years he had known him and Harrison still insisted on being called Mr Harrison rather than Charlie. The late night phone calls, the chauffeuring him short distances because of his limited mobility, he'd had enough of it.

Besides, the old man was losing his mind. Those ridiculous morning and evening swims that he claimed to enjoy. One of these days he would be found dead on that beach, the waves nibbling at his cold and withered corpse.

As for Johnny and Loaf, they were just a couple of filthy taigs from Tyrone, probably related to someone in the IRA. Where Andy came from, taigs were targets.

Back when he was young there used to be a game called 'The Only Good Catholic is a Dead Catholic' where you were either picked to be a member of the RUC or you were a Catholic.

If you were unlucky enough to be the latter and the RUC man caught you, he was allowed to give you a kicking before pretending to finish you off with a bullet to the head.

For some of his former classmates the schoolyard play-acting became the real thing in later life.

While Andy had dished out the odd hammering, he had never actually killed anyone. Not that he wouldn't, it was just a matter of circumstance.

The way Terry was talking he wouldn't have to get his hands bloodied on this occasion, the steel fixer sounded like he was perfectly happy to deal with Donnelly dumb and Donnelly dumber himself.

But no more servant boy, no more 'Yes Mr Harrison, no Mr Harrison'. It was time to become lord of the manor.

Glancing around him to make sure no one else on the site was watching, he held out his hand.

'Let's do it.'

JOHNNY stepped out as if he was checking the shutters when he was actually having a look to make sure all quarters were clear of prying eyes.

In his absence Terry and Andy hurriedly discussed the fact that Loaf had backed out of the night's mission.

'It's no big deal, one less body to get rid of,' whispered Terry. 'We stick to the plan. We claim that this clown pulled a move on us, turfed us out of his van and sped off, leaving us freezing at the roadside. In reality we tie him up, strangle him and chuck his corpse into the sea. In these winter tides he'll be halfway to the Caribbean before morning light.'

'And what about the Shaun boy, won't he be curious when his cousin vanishes into thin air?'

'He knows this guy's a fool, he told me as much that night we were out. He'll think that Johnny has come up with some half-arsed scheme to steal the drugs himself. Besides, what's he going to do, go to the cops and tell them that his cousin hasn't been seen since he went out to bring a massive haul of drugs on to the island? That he was supposed to be with him but that he chickened out at the last minute? Somehow I can't see it happening.'

When he was satisfied there was no one about, Johnny signalled to his accomplices to get into the van.

He fiddled with the heating system despite knowing that it had packed up months ago. While he did so, Andy went through the checklist one final time and outlined what the plan was.

Ropes, torches, life jackets, balaclavas, gloves, suitcases to put the drugs in – everything was ready.

The snow was continuing to fall heavily as they set off, the roads and paths now white in the blizzard-like conditions.

As they drove along Douglas prom the tracks made by the van were the only blemishes in the otherwise virgin blanket that was settling silently over the town.

Andy phoned Harrison to make sure the job was still on and that it wasn't being abandoned due to the inclement weather.

'It's all systems go guys,' he confirmed after being told that the mother ship was anchored and waiting for them.

No one spoke a word as they headed towards Castletown, a cocktail of nerves and adrenalin rendering each man mute.

To keep his mind from the rising tension Johnny thought about his cousin. They hadn't spoken since their fight.

Where was he right now? Was he sitting at home, wishing he hadn't backed out? Or was he comfortable in the warmth of his flat, happy to be far away from what was about to go down?

We could have done something together, thought Johnny as he drove. We could have used the money from Harrison's drugs to open a beach bar in Miami. How cool would that have been?

It all seemed so far away now.

He hadn't meant what he had said about Loaf being a stick in the mud. They were just different people. And he was right, he had stood up for him against the bullies.

Befriending that old man and taking him back to Derry one last time. Not in a million years would Johnny have been capable of such a selfless act.

Very few people would have been.

It was cold now, really cold. Glancing sideways at the two virtual strangers sitting as emotionless as concrete beside him, the feeling of unease that was gripping his gut tightened again.

What had he got himself into? Was Loaf right, were they going to double-cross him? Were they planning on harming him?

As they motored on towards their destination the dread only got heavier, weighing on him like a terrible black shroud. His eyes were starting to get sore from blinking.

How he wished he was somewhere else. How he would have loved to be in his cousin's apartment, the two of them watching Rocky IV for the hundredth time, drinking beer, laughing and cheering on the Italian Stallion as he chopped the machine-like Ivan Drago down to size.

But he wasn't in Loaf's apartment.

He was here, freezing, frightened and completely out of his depth.

Chapter Twenty Five

There was hardly a light on as the van made its way along Bridge Street.

Only a single window above The Anchor Bar was illuminated, most likely the landlord or landlady preparing for bed after a night at the pumps.

Under the ghostly gaze of Rushen Castle they pulled in close to the pier.

Despite their attempts to be as quiet as possible, the snow-covered night seemed to amplify every cough, every footstep, every closing door.

From where they were, they could see the rowboat bobbing in the harbour.

To their relief the blizzard had thinned and was falling now in flakes as fine as talcum powder.

Andy and Terry kitted up, pulling on life jackets, masks and gloves.

'You look like a couple of movie assassins,' Johnny joked as they prepared to leave him.

Neither of them laughed.

Andy messaged the mother ship to let them know they were on their way. Thirty seconds later an app on his phone let him know that the parcels were in the water.

'If you see anything, and I mean anything, you text me,' he hissed. 'Right Terry, let's go.'

They were going to have to row for about 30 minutes before they reached their cargo.

Including the time it would take to haul the drugs aboard, Johnny would have roughly an hour and 15 minutes to kill.

He watched as they made their way down the steps and into their craft.

Rather them than me, he thought, trapping his hands under his armpits in a bid to thaw his freezing fingers.

Silently they disappeared into the darkness.

Johnny climbed back into the van and began to fiddle again with the heating system. After poking a pen in through the grill for five minutes, to his amazement it started to work.

Confident that his heightened state of alert would prevent him from falling asleep, he pulled his jacket collar around his neck and prepared to wait.

He was wakened by the sound of someone rapping on the window.

Staring at him was a large middle-aged woman, wrapped up in winter coat and scarf.

Shocked at being torpedoed so abruptly out of dreamland, he wound the handle down.

'Are you alright son,' she said in a lilting Scottish accent. 'It's just that I saw you sleeping here in the van and thought you must be freezing on a bitter night like this.'

'I'm fine, thank you,' he replied, frantically trying to conjure up a good reason for his being where he was. 'I was working earlier and me and my mates decided to go to the pub afterwards, a sort of early Christmas party. I live in Kirk Michael and I didn't want to drive after a few pints. So I thought I would sleep them off here in the van.'

'That's like something my husband would do,' she chuckled. 'As long as you're okay, that's all.'

Johnny looked over her shoulder and out to sea. If Andy and Terry turned up now, they would all be in deep shit.

Thankfully there was no sign of them. The clock on the dashboard told him he had been asleep for 15 minutes.

'I'm fine, seriously. What are you doing out at this hour and in this weather,' he inquired as was the natural thing to do.

'Zeus here was barking the house down so I decided to take him for a wee walk. I must get back though, I have to be up for work in the morning. All the best son and fair play to you for not drink driving, there's far too much of that on this island.'

Johnny hadn't even noticed the dog. It was a little rat of a thing. Zeus. Aye, no bother missus.

'Okay, all the best and sleep tight,' he called with a smile as she started for home.

'Nosey old crow,' he mumbled as he wound the window back up and snorted a quick line to ensure he wouldn't drop off again.

An hour and a half later there was still no sign of the boat or its crew.

Starting to worry, he sent a text to make sure everything had gone smoothly.

TERRY was the main oarsman on account of him being the stronger of the two and so Andy could monitor the tracking system.

The bleeping on the phone got louder as they neared the stash.

The mother ship was long gone by the time they arrived. But the two bales were visible, a corner of each jutting out of the water.

As they pulled up alongside and got their hands on them, they realised they were bigger than either man had anticipated. Andy had done jobs like this before but nothing of this magnitude.

'Fuck sake,' said Terry. 'What do we do now?'

They talked briefly about one of them getting into the sea and trying to push the drugs up on to the boat by lifting them from underneath. The plan was quickly binned though on account of the cold and the unlikeliness of it actually working.

Instead they decided to try and lasso a rope around each block and haul it on board.

It took several attempts and three near capsizes but eventually they succeeded.

After a short breather, they set about lifting a bale to each end of the boat to balance it out.

On the return leg they shared rowing duties until finally Castletown harbour came into view.

On seeing them, Johnny reversed the van down the slipway and opened the rear doors.

He helped pull the boat on to dry land where they began to unburden it of its highly valuable load.

Andy and Terry clambered into the back of the van to begin transferring the packages of cocaine into the three suitcases they had brought with them.

'Turn that heating up Johnny,' called Terry. 'Not all of us have been sitting with our feet up all evening you know.'

With the drugs safely secreted and the cases zipped up, they set off.

Johnny and Andy had done a practice drive along the route that would take them to the Ramsey drop-off point.

What they had not factored into their planning were road signs covered in snow and a wintery blanket making every street look like the next.

It was going to be a slow journey.

Alone in the boat on their way out to pick up their collection, Andy and Terry had gone over their devious plot one more time.

On the way to Ramsey Terry would ask Johnny to pull over so he could pee. Once outside he would pretend the van had a flat tyre as a result of being weighed down by the drugs.

When Johnny stepped out to have a look, they would do him in.

'We dump his body in the sea, we hide the suitcases and we get rid of the van. You call Harrison in a panic and tell him we've been double-crossed.

'By the time Harrison's fit to do anything about it, especially in this weather, Johnny would have had plenty of time to get away. Harrison will assume he had a boat waiting to transport the gear to Ireland. You and I, we just play dumb, tell him we were caught completely off-guard, that we didn't expect for one second he would pull a gun on us.

'Then we sit tight until it's time to cash in.'

The matter of fact way Terry spoke about murder and dumping bodies in the sea sent a little flutter of goosebumps up Andy's arms. He had met cold-hearted men before but this guy, he was something else.

Terry meanwhile didn't give the slightest indication that he intended to commit two murders before daylight. There was only one person getting out of this alive and that was him.

With the drugs on board and the finishing line in sight, the mood inside the van was relaxed, jovial even. Where before hearts and stomachs had been as taut as cheese wire, now there was laughter, everyone calm, warm and happy to be on the road to easy street.

Terry had already picked his spot. He knew exactly where he was going to ask Johnny to pull in. And it was coming up in the next three minutes.

'I'm dying for a piss man,' he moaned theatrically. 'Any chance of you stopping for a minute, there's a lay-by up here around this next corner. I'll be done in a jiffy.'

'Can you not hold it in,' protested Johnny. 'We're almost there.'

'I can't, no. I'm literally going to piss myself here.'

'Okay, okay. But be quick,' he relented, oblivious to the fact that he was driving towards the last moments of his life.

Terry looked at Andy out of the side of his eye, telling him to be ready.

But just as they were about to put their plan into action, Johnny let out a roar.

'HOLY SHIT!'

'WHAT THE FUCK,' shouted Andy, his eyes wide, his face suddenly as white as the snow that was holding the fields on either side of them hostage.

In front of them was a sea of flashing blue lights.

Standing in the middle of the road waving a red and white beacon was a uniformed police officer.

Up ahead they could see an ambulance tending to some sort of accident.

This was not how it was supposed to work out.

The officer approached with a signal that indicated he wanted them to wind their window down.

'Good evening lads, or should that be morning,' he chuckled, glancing at his watch.

Tossing his head in the direction of the incident, he went on, 'What about this eh? An eejit on a motorcycle out in this weather. He's come around that corner there, lost control and slammed straight into the wall. He'll be in hospital for a while, that leg of his is like mashed potato.'

Shining the torch first on Johnny then on Andy, then on Terry, the friendly officer didn't appear to be suspicious. A local bobby on the beat lumbered with the night shift, he had probably been looking forward to spending his evening watching the telly and drinking tea.

'You lads may turn around and find an alternative route because this road is going to be closed all night.'

'Okay officer, no problem, we'll do that,' replied Johnny, trying to suppress the sense of panic he was feeling.

He began a three point turn, not an easy manoeuvre on a narrow, frozen country road.

Three points became five, then seven and then nine as he nudged the vehicle around. With only a few inches to go, their new friend came running back to them.

'I've just been speaking to my sergeant there and he told me to ask you, what are you lads doing out here at this hour? I suppose I should have asked that myself, shouldn't I,' he laughed again.

Horror gripped the three of them. They had prepared for every possibility except this one - A cover story should they be stopped.

'Mmmm, I'm taking these two to the airport,' stuttered Johnny.

'To the airport?'

'Yeah, they've a flight out in the morning. They're…they're just married and they're heading off on their honeymoon.'

If looks could kill Johnny Donnelly would have dropped dead right there and then.

Terry started shaking his head. What a fucking idiot.

'Married? Congratulations gentlemen,' nodded the no longer smiling officer, clearly starting to question the story he was being fed.

'Where's the honeymoon then?

'Benidorm,' said Andy, blurting out the first sunny destination that came to mind.

'Benidorm? Me and the wife went there a few years ago. Didn't think much of it to be honest.'

There was a ten second lull in conversation.

'See here's my problem lads. You're headed in the wrong direction for the airport. And besides, there's not a single chance of a plane getting off this island in this snow. I'm Peterson by the way, just in case you're wondering.'

They weren't.

Reaching for the radio that was pinned to his chest, Peterson requested the assistance of two colleagues.

'Just sit where you are a minute please. Once Jennings and Wylie get here, we're all going to step out of the van, nice and slow, do you hear me.'

The game was up. Terry thought about making a run for it. But ankle-deep in snow, he would be collared in seconds.

'Okay friends, out,' said Peterson. 'You, driver, open the back doors for me please.'

There was one final chance. It was slim but it was all they had. Confidence was going to be key.

Johnny pulled the doors back to reveal three suitcases. Exactly what a newly married couple would be taking on holiday with them.

'See, they're going on honeymoon just like I told you,' he announced boldly.

'And you know what, this is starting to feel like a witch hunt. Two Irish men and a Black fella pulled over and harassed by the police. I wonder what the newspapers would make of that officer Peterson. If you let us be on our way, you'll hear no more about it. But let me warn you, it's thin ice you're on, literally and...'

He didn't know what the next word should be so he left the end of the sentence hanging in the air.

It was a valiant attempt to wriggle out of the mess they found themselves in. And it might just have worked had it not been for the soaking wet life jackets, ropes and other equipment that made it look exactly like what it was.

'Open them up Jennings,' Peterson ordered, shining his torch on the cases.

As word filtered out about what might have been discovered, other officers left the crash scene and began to gather round.

Jennings drew back the zip with the caution of a bomb disposal expert.

When he flipped back the lid to expose the contents there was a collective gasp from the captivated audience.

Only three people were unsurprised at the big reveal.

'Benidorm did you say sir,' asked Peterson, producing a set of handcuffs from his waistband.

'By the looks of this, it'll definitely be all-inclusive where you're going. Unfortunately for you three, your hotel is going to have bars on the windows.'

Chapter Twenty Six

I write this book now from a distance of 19 years.

After being apprehended all three men pleaded guilty to importing narcotics with intent to sell and supply.

Andy and Terry got ten years each for their involvement in the operation.

Andy's solicitor somehow managed to negotiate an arrangement whereby he serve the second half of his sentence in Northern Ireland.

I never heard from him again and all being well I never will.

He was right about one thing. Charlie Harrison was found dead on his beach. It wasn't a heart attack that got him though, it was a bullet. Six months after the ill-fated smuggling plot he was discovered face down in the sand having taken a single shot to the head. Someone had to pay for the loss of the £8 million shipment I suppose. The cops never got anyone for his murder although I doubt they looked too hard.

Terry planned to return to London after serving his time. I know this because he wrote me a letter from prison telling me he still regarded me as a friend and that he was sorry about what had happened. He also told me about his tough childhood which did go some way to explaining how he became the man he did.

According to an article on the BBC news Terry Campbell died last year, stabbed in the heart while trying to steal a car.

Terry's story was never going to have a happy ending and I think he knew that himself.

Johnny, he got 12 years because he was driving the van. According to the judge it made him 'the ringleader of a sophisticated criminal network that was heaping misery on the good people of the Isle of Man'.

Johnny Donnelly and sophisticated. Words I never thought I would read in the same sentence.

Despite my asking him not to send me a prison invite in the event that he was caught, he did and I accepted. I visited him on many occasions during his incarceration, as did his parents.

He served eight years before being released early due to his good behaviour.

He's doing okay, still stumbling and tumbling through life, bouncing from one ill-conceived business venture to the next.

The last I heard he was living in Edinburgh where he has 'Donnelly's Disco', a mobile DJ set-up, on the road.

From what I'm told, he has managed to stay out of trouble since leaving jail. Here's hoping it stays that way but with Johnny, you just never know.

The Thirsty Sailor closed down soon after the arrests. I tried to keep it open but the bad press and the constant attention from the constabulary made it impossible to keep afloat.

I handed the keys back to the owner who put it up for sale. Eventually a property developer stepped in and took it off his hands.

It's an apartment block these days, each one with its own balcony looking out to the sea. You'll have to dig deep if you want to buy one though because they ain't cheap.

Gary 'Two Tellies' Morrison is still about. I met him quite recently when he tried to sell me a pair of Padidas trainers. They were the real thing apparently, but so-called because they were manufactured in Ireland.

Declan 'Knickers' McKenzie is still mooching about as well. He had another run-in with the police a few years back when he was caught with his trousers around his ankles on a bus.

I'm still waiting to turn on the television and see him being ushered from a police van into court with a blanket over his head. One of these days, just you wait and see.

Angie and Bert Russell are still together.

Bert is behaving himself, Angie is on the list for a new liver. If she gets it that'll be five between them. Someone get me the Guinness Book of Records on the phone.

Lilly Armstrong passed away many years ago. I would like to say I hope she's happy in heaven but I've a notion of going there myself one day. A more hellish prospect than listening to her singing for eternity I can't imagine.

Me? I have three lives now – one in Canada, one in the Isle of Man and one back home with mum in Ballyrush.

Abbey Vincent and I had six and a half wonderful years together.

After all the commotion I decided to take my mother's advice and go and see her.

From our Facebook correspondence I already knew she was special. But nothing could have prepared me for just how beautiful, smart and funny she was in real life.

Abbey fought so hard to stay but her illness finally took her in 2014. I miss her beyond measure but she lives on in our daughter Phoebe who thankfully has inherited her mother's brains and is not going to end up pulling pints like her old man.

Phoebe is excelling at school and already has plans to go to university where she hopes to study French and fine art. Her mum would have loved that.

I have her under strict instruction never to put me in a care home.

By some bizarre twist, Magnus's cottage in Peel came to me.

When they were clearing out his chalet they found a series of scribbled notes, one of them declaring me his 'best pal' and how it meant everything that I was taking him to Derry.

With his sister-in-law Winnie's written agreement, a judge ruled me to be his closest living relative.

His money, of which there was a significant amount, went to Sunny View Care Home.

I have the cottage rented out and I use the income to cover the mortgage on our home in Port Erin.

I made it to Tír na nÓg after all.

I took the liberty of adding Magnus's name to the bench in Peel which he had previously installed in Josie's memory.

On sunny days Phoebe and I get the bus over there and treat ourselves to ice cream. We sit on their bench and watch the fishermen land their catch.

If you ever make it to Port Erin, do pop in. You'll know our home by the sign at the gate that reads 'The Thirsty Sailor'.

I took it down before the bulldozers moved in.

To the best of my knowledge it's all the evidence there is to say the place ever existed.